AN UNUSUAL INHERITANCE

Eliza Ellis has a lot on her plate. Although she teaches part-time at the local school, her passion is for baking and cake decoration. When she inherits Lilac Cottage, much to everyone's surprise, she decides to move in rather than sell up. But she also inherits a sitting tenant, in the form of Greg Holt . . . When Eliza gets involved in a new baking enterprise in the village, old memories are stirred up — and Greg knows more than he is telling . . .

JEAN M. LONG

♦

AN UNUSUAL INHERITANCE

Complete and Unabridged

LINFORD
Leicester

First published in Great Britain in 2008

First Linford Edition
published 2018

A catalogue record for this book is available
from the British Library.

ISBN 978–1–4448–3617–2

Published by
F. A. Thorpe (Publishing)
Anstey, Leicestershire

Set by Words & Graphics Ltd.
Anstey, Leicestershire
Printed and bound in Great Britain by
T. J. International Ltd., Padstow, Cornwall

This book is printed on acid-free paper

1

There was a stunned silence as Eliza finished speaking and the full impact of her words sank in. Her family were looking at the letter in her hand.

At last her brother, James, said, 'But why, Eliza? Why would Great-Uncle Henry leave you his cottage? I mean, it wasn't as if he knew you or anything, and he was only related by marriage — not even a blood relation. So why you and not our cousin, Paul? After all, he is the oldest.'

Meryl Ellis took her daughter's arm. 'I think,' she said softly, 'it was probably because we named Eliza after his wife — your great-aunt Eliza.'

'Well, it's not very fair, is it?'

His father sighed, aware that James, despite approaching twenty-two, was still viewing things in black and white.

'Life isn't fair, James. The sooner you

1

learn that lesson, the better,' he told him, sternly.

'The thing is,' James pursued, 'Eliza didn't even get to meet Uncle Henry.'

'She did, actually, when she was about four,' his mother informed him.

Eliza, somewhat taken aback by her brother's reaction, said, 'I'm sorry you feel this way, James, but there's nothing I can do about it, is there?'

'You could always sell Lilac Cottage and share the proceeds,' James suggested. 'After all, it must be rather ramshackle and uninhabitable.'

'In which case, no-one would buy it, would they?' Eliza pointed out. 'Anyway, for your information, I'm planning to live in it.'

'You're what!' Her mother looked horrified. 'I'd advise you to think very carefully before you make any decisions like that, dear. Your great-uncle was practically a recluse, and the place is probably in a bit of a state.'

Eliza smiled to herself and said brightly, 'How about I make us all a

2

nice cup of tea, and then we'll feel a whole lot better about things. I promise to tell you all about Lilac Cottage after I've been to see it tomorrow.'

Meryl gasped. 'Tomorrow! So soon?'

Eliza went into the kitchen to make the tea. There was something she couldn't bring herself to tell her family at present. She felt a bit guilty harbouring a secret. Usually, she confided just about everything to them — but this was different. She hadn't wanted to hurt them, had been unsure of what their reactions might be and, now that things had taken such an unexpected turn, she needed to think it all through carefully.

'It was sad, that funeral,' Meryl said to James as they sat drinking tea. 'There were only a few of us there, James.'

'Well, I suppose if Great-Uncle Henry was a recluse then people took him at his word. Who else was there then, besides the three of you?'

'Oh, there were only a handful of others, and of course the vicar and pall bearers.'

3

'Who were these others then?' James persisted, helping himself to a piece of shortbread.

'One was Mr Hughes, Henry's solicitor,' his father put in. 'He made a point of seeking us out and introducing himself.'

'He was very pleasant,' Meryl added. 'He told us that one of the women there had been Henry's home help, and that there were also a couple of representatives from his publishers present — you remember I told you he was a writer?'

'Other than that, we don't know who they were,' his father continued. 'Everyone was invited back to Lilac Cottage for refreshments after the service, but we decided to get back here. It was all a bit awkward really. After all, we hadn't seen Henry for years.'

'Well, let's hope he's at peace now,' Meryl said. 'He wasn't a happy man — not after Eliza died. Anyway, I'm glad we kept in touch. We always sent him a Christmas card. I think your great-aunt would have liked that.'

Eliza smiled to herself, feeling sure that Great-Uncle Henry had liked the gesture too, even though he hadn't reciprocated.

'I take it you've told that boyfriend of yours about the inheritance, Liza?' her father asked, stirring his tea vigorously.

'Absolutely! I phoned him just after I received the letter. He's pleased for me, of course,' Eliza told him. 'He's arranged to meet me at the cottage later on tomorrow. He's got a play rehearsal first thing at school which he can't get out of. The performance is looming ever nearer.'

Although she spoke lightly, she'd been bitterly disappointed when Kelvin had suddenly remembered this. They spent little enough time together as it was, so their weekends were precious.

'You teachers are so hard-working,' her mother sympathised.

'Huh! Think about all the holidays they get,' James snorted. 'Anyway, Liza only works two days a week.'

'Hardly! It's not like I'm resting on

my laurels the rest of the time,' his sister pointed out. 'Anyway, how would I manage to help Dad in the bakery *and* find time for my cake-making business if I took on any more teaching?'

'I thought cookery was compulsory now,' James commented, helping himself to more shortbread.

'Yes, in an ideal world it would be — in schools where they've got the proper facilities and the right amount of trained staff. But Food Technology is still not available to everyone yet. In our school it's only for the younger students.'

'Would you like a full-time teaching job?' her father asked anxiously.

Eliza shook her head. 'No, Dad. I enjoy helping you and having my own business far too much. If anything, I'd like to expand it.'

'Your teaching provides you with your bread and butter, doesn't it, dear,' her mother jested and everyone laughed, although that particular joke had worn a bit thin.

Later, as Eliza got ready for bed in her small room under the eaves, she thought about her visit to Lilac Cottage the following day and was filled with a mixture of excitement and trepidation. She only hoped Kelvin would feel the same way as she did about the cottage.

Eliza had met Kelvin Summers almost two years ago when he had joined the staff at the school where she worked. They'd had rather an on-off relationship, partly because both of them were still living at home. She hoped that once he'd seen the cottage and realised there was the prospect of a place of their own, then he might suggest making their relationship more permanent. Admittedly, he hadn't mentioned marriage; in fact, they were just cruising along, so perhaps it was up to her to make the first move.

On an impulse, she picked up her phone and dialled his number. After all, it wasn't that late.

Kelvin didn't seem pleased to hear her voice.

'Eliza, whatever's wrong? Why are you phoning me at this time of night?'

She felt as if he'd thrown cold water over her.

'Nothing's wrong. I just felt like having a chat. Also, I wanted to remind you about tomorrow.'

'Tomorrow?' He sounded blank.

'Come on, Kelvin — surely you can't have forgotten already! We're going to Rushden to look at the cottage. The one I've just inherited, in case it's slipped your mind.'

'What? No — no, how could it? You only told me about it at lunch time. It's just that . . . ' He hesitated. 'Actually, I'm a bit tied up tomorrow.'

'You've told me about the rehearsal,' Eliza said impatiently. 'So, what else?'

There was a pause and, in the background, she distinctly heard female laughter.

'Kel, where are you? Are you with someone? Shall I ring you back?'

'No, it's OK,' he assured her. 'I've been for a drink with some mates of mine — you wouldn't know them. We meet up periodically for a drink and a chat . . . Look, I've got to go now, but I'll give you a ring tomorrow morning, OK?'

Eliza didn't know what to think. Who were these people he was with? She thought she knew most of Kelvin's friends, so why hadn't he mentioned these ones before?

She realised there were still areas of his life she knew nothing about and wished he'd be more open with her. And why wouldn't he make a more definite arrangement about visiting the cottage? She thought he'd have been more enthusiastic, but he'd sounded as if he couldn't have cared less.

* * *

Eliza had a restless night and got up early to put the finishing touches to a wedding cake she was delivering that morning. As she came out of the bathroom, she found her brother waiting impatiently on the landing.

'Morning Liza. So, are you and Kelvin planning to set up home together in this cottage of yours?'

She glared at him. 'Absolutely none of your business! We haven't even been to see it yet, so don't you go jumping to conclusions!'

He grinned at her. 'You're very touchy this morning. You two haven't fallen out, have you?'

'Enough, James! You'd better use the bathroom before someone else wants it. Some of us have got work to do.'

James grimaced. 'Ouch! Someone got out of bed on the wrong side! Actually, I'm off to that motorbike rally today, with Steve.'

'Oh, yes. Well, just be careful.'

'I know what I'm doing, Liza. I've been riding a bike for a few years now.'

She touched his arm affectionately. 'All the same, just be careful.'

'I will if you will! After all, you're going to be poking around in some grotty old cottage that hasn't seen the light of day for yonks. Probably full of spiders and mice and loose floor-boards.'

Eliza threw her slipper at him. He ducked and laughingly disappeared into the bathroom. If only he knew, she thought, as she hurriedly dressed in jeans and a tunic top. Of course, she'd have to tell her family and Kelvin that she wasn't exactly a stranger to Lilac Cottage but, for the moment, it was her secret — just until she'd decided what to do about her inheritance.

* * *

The drive to Rushden, situated in the Weald of Kent, was through a beautiful stretch of countryside along pleasant, narrow lanes where the thin February sun filtered through the hedgerows. She caught sight of a pheasant in a nearby field, and took a deep breath in as she drove.

Eliza enjoyed her life but, just recently, she'd been feeling a bit

11

restless. She knew it was because her relationship with Kelvin didn't seem to be going anywhere. Most of her friends were married or in long term relationships, but Kelvin seemed perfectly content with the way things were.

Eliza sighed. She could see herself working in the same school in twenty years' time, when her parents had long since retired from their bakery business in Bembury. Her thoughts turned to Great-Uncle Henry. Curiosity had overcome her one summer, about three years ago. She had a friend who was mad keen on her family tree and it had got Eliza interested in her own. Eliza had thought that perhaps Henry would be able to fill her in with a few details about her great-aunt Eliza, whose namesake she was, and the bakery which used to be in Rushden and had once belonged to the Ellis family.

Henry Curtis hadn't replied to her letter and so, on an impulse, she had decided to call on the elderly gentleman unannounced. His home-help had opened the door but — on that occasion — he hadn't been prepared to see Eliza.

Undaunted, she'd returned a couple of days later and, going round to the back of the cottage, had found her great-uncle sitting in the garden. At first, he'd seemed startled by her presence and had been reluctant to speak to her, but Eliza could be very persuasive when she chose.

She grinned. Henry Curtis had turned out to be quite a character and the two of them had forged a strange kind of friendship over the past years. He had insisted, however, that she kept it quiet — said he didn't want the whole family descending on him and that, anyway, he was a writer and preferred a solitary existence. He had taken to contacting Eliza periodically and arranging for her to visit.

Eliza approached Lilac Cottage with very mixed feelings now that the old man had died. She passed the house where Kerry Jones, who had been Henry's immediate neighbour and home-help, lived. Eliza would have felt happier if Kelvin had been there with her. Recently, she'd become aware that he could be rather insensitive and unreliable — his absence on this occasion was a case in point.

Lilac Cottage stood alone, along a lane with grass verges dotted with snowdrops. The cottage was built of Kentish ragstone. It was much bigger than it looked from the outside, due to an extension at the back. Eliza smiled as she imagined what her family's reaction would be when they saw the state-of-the-art kitchen.

Great-Uncle Henry might have been something of a recluse during the last few years of his life, but he certainly liked his creature comforts and was happy for alterations to be made, providing he could retire to the summer house in the garden and leave everyone else to get on with it.

There was a parking space behind the

cottage and Eliza quickly found the right key to the kitchen door. Before she explored she intended to have a cup of coffee. She'd brought a few provisions in her backpack. She'd expected it to be cold inside but, to her surprise, the range was alight and she could hear the fridge chuntering away. She opened it and was amazed to see fresh milk and juice in the door and, on the shelves, eggs and a tray of lamb chops still well within date. There were fresh vegetables, fruit and salad stuff too.

A shiver of apprehension ran through her. Supposing someone was squatting? Just then she heard the sound of barking and, a moment later, a springer spaniel nearly knocked her over, yelping excitedly.

'Gyp! Hello, boy.' She stroked his silky brown and white coat and looked up to see who was with Henry's dog. A tall, slimly-built man with a crop of tousled dark hair appeared in the kitchen doorway. He didn't look like a squatter.

'Hallo. I wasn't expecting you,' he greeted her.

'And I most certainly wasn't expecting you,' Eliza rejoined, feeling at a distinct disadvantage. To her relief, she recognised the man as having been at the funeral, although he looked decidedly different in his casual attire. 'Are you one of Great-Uncle Henry's neighbours?'

A flicker of surprise crossed the man's good-looking features.

'No, I'm Greg — Gregory Holt. Down, Gyp!'

His name meant absolutely nothing to her, although he obviously thought it should.

'I heard someone was looking after the dog. Are you caretaking as well?' Eliza asked curiously.

His grey eyes widened. 'I take it you haven't spoken to Henry's solicitor yet?'

'Well, no,' she said uncertainly. 'That is — only on the phone, and very briefly at the funeral. He was in court when I called for the keys, but his P.A. was expecting me when I went to sign for them.'

'Right. Well, just give me a few minutes whilst I rub this dog down — he's been in the stream — and then I'll explain the situation. Help yourself to coffee from the percolator. Mine's white with one sugar,' he grinned, cheekily.

Eliza thought of the sachets of instant coffee she'd put in her backpack, together with the carton of long-life milk, and looked around for the percolator.

Gregory Holt returned shortly afterwards. 'There are some biscuits in that tin. Now, I think I'd better attempt to fill you in — although probably Mr Hughes should be the one to do that.'

Eliza looked at him expectantly.

Greg Holt gave a slight smile. 'Henry always referred to me as his secretary.'

Eliza frowned in confusion. 'His secretary!' she echoed, trying to make sense of this. 'But why would he need a secretary?'

Greg sipped his coffee. 'That's better — Henry always insisted on good coffee . . . Did you know he was a historian?'

'Of course I did. He used to lecture at the college, years back.'

'And did you also know he wrote books?'

'I was aware he'd written one or two historical biographies, yes.'

Feeling impatient she wondered where this conversation was leading.

'Rather more than that. Anyway, as time went on, he found it increasingly difficult to sit at the computer — so he dictated, and I acted as his scribe. I realise people thought he was a recluse, and so he was, to a degree, but he learnt to trust me. And I helped him out in various other ways too.'

'Like a carer?' she asked, trying to understand what he was telling her.

Greg nodded and pushed the biscuit tin towards her.

'I suppose I was a sort of general factotum. Amongst other things, I organised all the alterations to the cottage for him. Henry didn't mind what was done downstairs, so long as no-one encroached on his domain upstairs — except for myself and, when necessary, the doctor or nurse.'

'Right. So what exactly is your role now that my great-uncle's no longer here?' Eliza asked, puzzled.

'Henry left a sum of money in the hands of the solicitor to pay my wages until his last book is finished — together with some . . . er . . . other matters that he's asked me to deal with.'

She was taken aback. 'I don't understand. Are you saying you're going to be allowed to finish his book?'

He smiled at her. 'Got it in one! All the notes are there, many of them recorded. The bulk of the research is done, so now I only have to check out a few details and type it up. Henry's editor is happy for me to email it to him chapter by chapter. And I'll be staying here while I do it.'

Eliza drank her coffee as she tried to

get her head round this.

'OK, but why do you have to work from here? Surely you could do it equally as well from your own home?'

'Well, for one thing, all Henry's papers and books are in his study. And, quite apart from that, this *is* my home; has been for the last few years.'

Eliza drew herself up to her full height of five foot four inches and glared at him. 'Well, I shall see what Mr Hughes has to say about that. Anyway, if that's the case, why haven't I ever encountered you here before when I've visited Great-Uncle Henry?'

He laughed. 'Your uncle was a rather devious gentleman. He made sure that he kept us apart. Every time you arranged to call, he gave me strict instructions to make myself scarce. I think he wanted to keep the myth going that he was a recluse. You were favoured, you know. One of the very few people he deigned to see during the last few years of his life. And I think there were other reasons for not letting us meet. I rather think he was afraid that one or the other of us might say something out of turn.'

Eliza frowned. 'How d'you mean?'

'He didn't want his affairs discussed whilst he was still alive and, unfortunately, had grown suspicious of everyone.'

'I see,' she said, although she didn't really see at all. 'Well, once I've spoken with Mr Hughes, I can decide on the best course of action. How long do you think it'll take you to finish the book?'

He shrugged. 'How long is a piece of string? I have absolutely no idea. As long as it takes, I suppose. Personally, I would have thought you'd have been happy to have someone here in the role of caretaker, and to look after poor old Gyp.'

'But surely you must take some time off,' Eliza said, as it suddenly dawned on her that Kelvin was hardly likely to be interested in Lilac Cottage once he discovered Greg was still living there.

To her annoyance, Greg looked amused.

'Well, naturally. Since Henry's died I organise my working day to suit myself. At present, I seem to have more time on my hands than I've been used to for a long while.'

'Good, then you'll be able to get the book finished more quickly, won't you?' she said tartly. 'I'm hoping to move in here as soon as possible and, somehow, I don't think there'll be room for both of us.'

Greg surveyed her, looking more amused than ever.

'On the contrary, I would have thought there was plenty of space — you don't seem overly big to me.'

Before she could think of a suitable retort, he whistled to Gyp, who shot out of the utility room wagging his tail; they disappeared through a door leading into the hall.

Feeling distinctly cross, Eliza decided to check out the cupboards. They were all in apple-pie order. The shelves were stacked with a variety of cans of tinned food, and there were packets and jars of basic commodities. A sudden thought struck her. Perhaps Greg Holt didn't live here alone. Perhaps he had a girlfriend.

Eliza hadn't seen over the entire cottage before. She decided not to wait for Kelvin any longer, but to go on a little exploration on her own. Besides the utility room and a downstairs cloakroom, there was a large, walk-in pantry, the sitting-room where she used to meet with her great-uncle, and a dining-room. She was just about to go upstairs when Kelvin phoned.

'Sorry, Liza, the rehearsal's gone on much longer than I expected. I'm afraid I'm not going to make it to Rushden now. Sorry to cry off, but if I can do a couple of hours' work this afternoon, we could meet up this evening for a drink and some food.'

Eliza was bitterly disappointed. She'd so wanted Kelvin to visit the cottage so that she could see his reaction.

Climbing the stairs, she went to look at Henry's bedroom. She decided it was rather dark and gloomy, but it definitely had potential. There were three other doors on the landing. One she knew to be a bathroom, and she supposed another one to be the study Greg Holt had referred to, so the third had to be his bedroom.

As she hesitated, wondering if she dared take a look, one of the doors opened and Greg came out.

'You're still here, then. Want to see Henry's study and library?'

He stood back so that she could go in. It was an impressive room with book-lined shelves and a huge mahogany desk. By the window was a state-of-the-art computer, and an enormous stack of files and papers were piled on a nearby table.

There were paintings and framed photographs on the walls. Over the fireplace hung a portrait of a young woman in a turquoise dress. She crossed to look at it, aware that it had to be of her great-aunt Eliza, and gasped as she realised the portrait bore a striking resemblance to herself. The same oval face and creamy skin; the same fair hair and green eyes. It was uncanny — like looking at herself in a mirror.

'Yes, it's amazing how alike you are, although I believe Henry's wife was rather more petite.'

Eliza bristled. 'There's no need to be personal!'

'She was probably more even-tempered, too,' Greg added.

'That's because she didn't get to meet you,' Eliza rejoined, and he grinned infuriatingly.

'There's another floor above this one, a large attic room that I use as my sitting-room. My bedroom's opposite this room, and the bathroom's to the left. Henry had an en-suite put in his room many years back.'

'Oh, I'm not sure I'd fancy sleeping in his room. It's a bit gloomy for my liking,' she told him.

'You could have a point there, but you obviously haven't found Eliza's little den.'

He'd captured her interest and she followed him from the study and back into Henry's bedroom where, almost hidden by the dark wallpaper, was another door at the side of the bed. Greg pushed it open and she caught her breath as she entered for, despite the fact that it was very small and, at present, devoid of furniture except for a day bed and a tiny walnut bureau, it was flooded with sunlight and utterly charming — although it obviously hadn't had much done to it since Eliza's day.

'What d'you think?'

'It's delightful,' she told him. 'I wouldn't have known it existed.'

'So would that solve the problem?'

It was obvious he wasn't going to give way and offer to move out of his room, nor was he going to show it to her. In the short term, she supposed this little room would do, but if she and

Kelvin were to set up home here then she'd need to think again.

'I'll be back again next week when I've seen Mr Hughes,' she said firmly.

'I'll look forward to it,' Greg told her and gave her a devastating smile.

* * *

'I wish I'd have been there. I'd have soon sorted him out,' Kelvin said when they met up that evening.

'And what exactly would that have achieved?' Eliza asked him, wishing he wasn't quite so quick-tempered.

'You're not going to take this sitting down, are you? It's your cottage now. If you don't want this chap staying there then throw him out.'

Eliza sighed. 'It's not that straightforward, Kel. Until I've seen my great-uncle's solicitor, I don't know all the facts. But for now, Greg Holt's doing a pretty good job of caretaking, and there's Uncle Henry's dog to think about.'

Kelvin's pale-blue eyes narrowed.

'You always were too soft for your own good, Liza. Anyway, just as soon as this fellow's gone, you can put the place on the market.'

Eliza picked up her wine glass. 'Who said anything about putting it on the market?' she demanded. 'The more I see of Lilac Cottage, the more I like it. I've absolutely no intention of selling it. Oh Kelvin, I can't wait for you to see it. It's a dream home.'

Kelvin stared at her, and she was uncomfortably aware that she'd sounded too enthusiastic.

'So it's true then? Your brother said that's what you'd got in mind.'

'James? When did you get to speak to him?' she asked, a sinking feeling in her stomach.

'This morning, actually. I saw him in the middle of town; he was just about to set off with his mates for the rally.'

Her cheeks burned as she wondered what else James might have said to Kelvin. 'He had no right telling you anything until I'd had a chance to speak to you. It's a lovely place, really quaint. Kelvin, can't you come with me to take a look tomorrow?'

He shook his head. 'Regretfully, no. I've promised to take my mother to my sister's for lunch and then, when I get back, I've got the usual mountain of coursework to mark.'

'Next weekend?' she asked, hopefully.

'I'm sorry, Liza, but until this play is out of the way, I haven't got too much time for socialising. A quick drink or a visit to the gym is about all I can manage at the moment.'

'I see,' she said in such a disappointed tone that he patted her hand.

'I'm not sure that you do. That's what real teaching is all about — commitment.'

Eliza felt stung. 'What do you mean by *real* teaching? Are you insinuating that Food Technology isn't in the same league as your Drama and English classes?'

'No, of course not. Just that you're

only part-time, and that's a bit different.'

'I don't see how. I still attend parents' evenings, staff meetings and other functions. *And* I work another couple of days a week in my father's bakery. To say nothing of fitting in my own work in between.'

Kelvin grinned. 'Oh, come on, Eliza! Making cakes can hardly be classed as hard work!'

Eliza was incensed. 'How would you know?' she demanded. 'I bet you've never made a cake in your life.'

'Actually, I'm a dab hand at flapjacks,' he told her and laughed infuriatingly.

For two pins she would have poured her wine over him.

'For your information, at the moment, I'm making a wedding cake for a customer who wants three tiers — one sponge, one fruit, and one chocolate. In case you hadn't realised, I also make the decorations — rosebuds, butterflies, whatever the customer wants. You should try it sometime. You can't do sugar-craft in five minutes.'

'OK, keep your hair on. I retract that comment.' He drained his glass. 'Anyway, to go back to this cottage of yours. It's a bit of a pig in a poke, isn't it? I mean, if you don't want to sell it and this bloke Holt's living in it then . . . '

'I intend to live in it, too,' she told him firmly, and realised, from his look of utter astonishment, that this was the very last thing he'd expected her to say.

Later, when Kelvin kissed her goodnight, he seemed distant and Eliza wondered what was on his mind.

2

The following week Eliza saw Mr Hughes who told her more or less the same as Greg Holt, but in more detail. It seemed her options were either to move into Lilac Cottage alongside Greg, rent it out to someone acceptable to Greg, or wait until he'd moved on and then put it on the market.

She was still mulling things over, and was both pleased and surprised when Kelvin volunteered to go with her to see the cottage that Sunday. Apparently, his mother had arranged to have lunch with friends and he'd decided he needed a breather from work.

Also, he readily agreed to accompany her to a Valentine's dinner and dance at a local hotel, when she produced the complimentary tickets her father had been given.

She'd rung Greg Holt to let him

know him they'd be coming over, and he'd told her he wouldn't be around for most of Sunday, so that solved another problem, although she couldn't help feeling a slight twinge of disappointment. Anyway, it saved any unpleasantness from Kelvin, who was likely to just have a go at him.

They arrived at Lilac Cottage mid-morning. It had been a frosty start to the day, but now the sun was shining brightly. The cottage looked more picturesque than ever. Kelvin parked the car and looked about him, lips pursed.

'Bit isolated, isn't it? Stuck in the back of beyond with only one other house in sight. Not so decrepit as I'd imagined, though, at least from the outside.'

The green spikes of myriad daffodils were already poking their way through the soil and Eliza knew it would be a picture in spring. She took a deep breath, surveying the scene with plea-sure. This time she decided to use the front entrance and, after struggling with the lock, led the way into the small hall.

Kelvin followed her inside and stood looking about him critically.

'It's a bit gloomy, isn't it? Could do with a lick of paint.'

Eliza chose to ignore this remark and, pushing open the sitting-room door, waited for his reaction.

'Hmm — rather too much brown furniture for my liking. You'd need to look out for the woodworm. This room's got potential though, I'll give it that, even if it is old-fashioned. The wood-burning stove's a good feature.'

She was stung by his comments and said defensively, 'But the furnishings have got to be in keeping with the cottage. Too much modern stuff would look totally out of place in here.'

They moved on to the dining-room, but Kelvin didn't show much interest until they reached the kitchen. He whistled.

'Wow! This is more like it. My mother would certainly approve of this.

Every conceivable mod-con! Surprising, eh? OK, show me the rest of this place and then I'm taking you out to lunch.'

'Oh, let's have coffee first and then, after you've seen over the cottage, we can take a proper look at the garden. There's a summer house out the back where my great-uncle used to do his writing — until he became ill.'

Kelvin shivered. 'Not on a February day! Anyway, I can see most of it from the window. So come on — lead the way upstairs. I'm curious to see this study you've mentioned.'

Disappointingly, however, the door had a security lock on the outside and she didn't know the code.

Kelvin looked irritated. 'Got a bit of a nerve, this Holt fellow, hasn't he? it's your cottage now, so you ought to be able to go wherever you choose.'

'Oh, he's probably just being responsible. After all, there's a lot of valuable computer equipment in there.'

Eliza had secretly hoped that the door

to Greg's room would be unlocked, but it wasn't.

Kelvin frowned. 'Who does he think he is? He's the guest in your cottage, not the other way round.'

'Oh, I don't blame him really. He's probably got some valuables in there, too.'

Eliza didn't doubt that one of the house keys might fit, but was determined not to pry. She jangled the bunch of keys.

'One place I haven't been is up in the attic. Apparently, that's been turned into Greg's private sitting-room. I can't think he'd object to us having a look in there.'

'Eliza, this is your cottage so he's no right to object to you going anywhere you want.'

The sitting-room had been left open and it was amazingly big.

'Wow! What a view! Oh look, Kel, there's a swing under the apple tree and there are sheep in the orchard beyond the hedge.'

But Kelvin seemed more interested in the television set and music equipment.

'Can't be short of a bob or two, this lodger fellow!'

'Perhaps my great-uncle paid for it.' She was looking at the book-lined walls and trying to determine what Greg's taste in reading might be.

Opening a cupboard, Kelvin revealed quantities of CDs.

'He's obviously got a highbrow taste,' he remarked. 'Mainly classical, although there's a bit of jazz and some country and western thrown in for good measure.'

There were some tasteful prints on the walls too, and one or two photographs on a shelf. Eliza couldn't resist peering at the photographs to see if she could find any clue about the man sharing her cottage, but they were just ordinary family groups; Gregory in cap and gown on his graduation day, obviously with his parents and a girl — a sister or a girlfriend, she wondered.

Kelvin was looking bored. He pulled her to him in a tight embrace and kissed her hard.

'I've got the general impression of this place,' he told her, 'so let's go back downstairs.'

Eliza hesitated. She was bitterly disappointed at his lack of interest. She hadn't even show him Henry's room or Eliza's den.

He caught her hand. 'Come on. We'll take a quick look round the garden and then we'll go to the Drunken Duck for lunch.'

* * *

The Drunken Duck, a pub in the nearby village, was divided into a series of alcoves and cosy eating areas. As Eliza walked past one of them, she was amazed to see Greg Holt seated at a table in the company of an elegant young woman with silver-blonde hair, who Eliza recognised from the funeral.

Suddenly, Greg looked up and their

eyes met. He raised his hand in acknowledgement. Kelvin didn't notice because he was marching ahead looking for a table.

Eliza was intrigued. Greg might have spent the last few years in a fairly isolated environment, but he'd obviously found time to socialise. Apparently, he didn't lead the bachelor existence she'd assumed. She wondered who his companion was, and if her great-uncle had met her.

'So, what d'you think?' Eliza asked as they began their roast. 'About the cottage, I mean.'

'I think you're a lucky girl to have inherited that neat little package at your age. Obviously, it would make things easier if that guy, Holt, hadn't come along as part of the deal. I suppose you could have a bit of a wait on your hands before he vacates the premises.'

'Oh, there's plenty of room for two or even three people in that cottage,' she said, careful not to look at him.

He gave her a fleeting glance.

'Yes, but who's going to want to live there with an unknown lodger?'

'So what would you do — in my shoes?' she asked, trying to sound casual.

'Try to think of some way of getting him out of my property, I guess — like having loud parties or inviting a couple of noisy friends to move in.'

She laughed. 'Be serious! What good would that do? No, I'm just going to have to abide by the terms of the will and sit it out. Come on — let's have your honest opinion on the matter.'

Kelvin finished his mouthful of Yorkshire pudding.

'OK, if all else failed, I'd have to wait until the guy left of his own accord and then I'd put it on the market.'

'So, you wouldn't want to move in — have your own space?' she asked, swallowing her disappointment.

He was dissecting a roast potato and didn't look up immediately.

'Why would I? I'm perfectly happy living where I am and Lilac Cottage is too much out in the sticks for me.'

'Right,' she said dully, as her dreams finally disintegrated. 'Don't you want to be independent? Settle down?'

He frowned. 'One day, when I'm about forty perhaps, but for the moment, I'm fine where I am.'

'A few months ago you seemed to be champing at the bit to have a place of your own,' she reminded him, unable to understand his change of heart.

'Mmm, but things have changed, haven't they? My sister's married now, and if I moved out, my mother would be on her own. I can't just swan off and leave her.'

'Right. Well, I'm thinking of moving into the cottage anyway,' Eliza told him, somewhat defiantly.

Kelvin cut into his roast beef. 'You're in a different position from me. You're living in that cramped little house, whereas I've got my own rooms in a large detached property with everything I could wish for.'

Eliza had been looking forward to the

meal, but suddenly had no appetite. She realised now just how selfish Kelvin could be. She pushed her plate to one side and took a sip of wine.

'Just imagine the cottage was yours. If you sold it and didn't want to move into another property, what would you spend the money on?'

He laughed. 'Oh, that's easy — a sports car, exotic holidays. Maybe put some by. But that's a hypothetical situation. You're the one who's inherited a cottage, not me. Looking at it from my angle, why would I want to move out of a perfectly good home, even if the opportunity arose? My meals are on the table each evening, my laundry's done for me, and my rooms are cleaned. It's better than being in a first-class hotel. No, I'm quite content with my life as it is.'

It was at that moment Eliza knew she was going to move into Lilac Cottage and carve out a new life for herself — with or without Kelvin Summers.

* * *

'You can't be serious!' James said to his sister, incredulously. 'Mum, Dad — tell me this isn't happening.'

Meryl looked at her daughter.

'Are you sure, dear? I mean, now that you've seen the solicitor and discussed the terms of the will with him, wouldn't you be better to sit tight and wait until Gregory Holt vacates Lilac Cottage?'

Her father said nothing, but Eliza could tell from the set of his shoulders that he was annoyed with her. She touched his arm.

'You haven't said anything, Dad. Would you really mind if I went to live in Lilac Cottage?'

'You must do what you like, Eliza,' he told her stiffly. 'You've disappointed me. I didn't think you could be so deceitful.'

'Whatever do you mean?' Eliza demanded, stung by this remark.

'To think that a daughter of mine could go behind my back and visit that

. . . that man, is beyond my comprehension. He did things that brought shame on our family and damaged its reputation, Eliza! No wonder he left you that cottage. It was to ease his conscience!'

And, scooping up his newspaper, he hurried from the room.

'Oh dear!' her mother said. 'You've properly upset your father now.'

Eliza was bemused. 'But I don't understand what I did that was so very wrong. I just visited an old gentleman to find out more about his wife, whose namesake I am.'

'But you went behind our backs. Keeping it to yourself all this time and only telling us a few days ago! Surely you must have realised we wouldn't have approved?'

'It honestly wasn't like that, Mum. I didn't tell you because I was asked not to by Great-Uncle Henry. And how could I have known you wouldn't approve, when I have no idea what it is that he did to upset you all?'

Her mother shrugged. 'Oh, I'm afraid he just wasn't a very nice person, Liza. He upset a great many people besides us, including your grandmother and several of the families who were employed in the Rushden bakery at the time. Anyway, it's best forgotten — no point raking up the past, especially as Henry is dead. No good can come of it.'

'Can you just explain it to me again? How come Great-Aunt Eliza inherited the bakery and not our grandfather?' James asked, looking puzzled.

'Oh, that's because your great-grandfather outlived your grandfather by a number of years. Your grandfather was seriously wounded in the war and died a few years after returning from the battlefield. When your great-grandfather became ill, Eliza took over the running of the bakery. Whilst your grandmother helped out as much as she could, she had your dad and Uncle Fred to look after, and her heart simply wasn't in it. Fortunately, your father and your uncle Fred were happy to work in the bakery as soon as they left school.'

James continued to look puzzled. 'But I still don't understand why the Rushden bakery was sold when Great-Aunt Eliza died.'

'Can we drop it?' Eliza pleaded. 'I've had enough for one day.' She turned to her mother. 'I'm sorry if I've upset you and Dad. It was the last thing I intended, but my mind's made up. I'm going to move into Lilac Cottage as soon as possible.'

★ ★ ★

Eliza was tidying up the Food Technology room after a group of exuberant twelve-year-olds had spent the morning baking, when she got a message asking her to see the head teacher.

Jane Mitchell, an elegant woman in her forties, asked Eliza to sit down, and carried on writing for a few moments. Eliza nervously racked her brain trying to think of anything she might have done wrong.

Finally, Mrs Mitchell looked up and Eliza saw that, unusually, the head-teacher seemed uncomfortable.

'Has Donna had the opportunity to speak to you, Eliza?'

Eliza hadn't seen the other half of her job-share team so far that week.

'No, but I'm expecting to see her later on today at the departmental meeting. Has something happened?'

Jane Mitchell hesitated. 'Donna's husband has been offered promotion and, unfortunately, it means them moving out of the area. The thing is, Eliza, I need to fit more Food Technology into the timetable for the younger students, so it would make more sense to advertise the post as full-time. Would you be prepared to up your hours? I realise you might have a problem because of your other inter-ests.'

For a moment, Eliza sat and stared at her hands. Much as she enjoyed her two days each week teaching, the last thing she wanted was a full timetable.

She swallowed. 'I'm sorry, Jane, I'm afraid you've taken me rather by surprise. Wouldn't you be prepared to consider another job share?' she asked.

The older woman sighed. 'Oh dear, Eliza, you are putting me in an awkward position. We don't want to lose you, my dear, but the school must come first and — to be blunt — I sometimes feel that my part-timers don't always appear to be as dedicated as my full-time staff.'

Eliza controlled her temper with a great deal of difficulty.

'I think that is rather an unjust comment, Mrs Mitchell. I put in a lot of extra hours over and above my two days a week.'

Jane Mitchell's eyes were steely.

'But the fact remains that you need to sort out your priorities. Do you want to concentrate on your teaching career? Or helping your father in his bakery, or even your own cake-making enterprise?

What's it to be? There is a question of commitment, Eliza.'

★ ★ ★

Kelvin found Eliza sitting in a corner of the staff-room, moodily staring into space.

'Hey, what's up Liza? You look as if you've lost a fiver and found fifty pence.'

'Jane Mitchell seems to have issued me with an ultimatum. Oh, you might as well know.'

She told him briefly what had transpired and he whistled.

'Much as I hate to say it, I suppose she does have a point.'

Eliza stared at him uncomprehendingly. 'How d'you mean?'

'What she said about commitment. It *is* different working here day in and day out, you know. It's like being a part of a large family. You can't get the whole picture if you flit in and flit out.'

'Thanks, Kel. I thought I could count

on you for support, but obviously I thought wrong!'

'Liza — I'm sorry if that sounded a bit harsh. It's just that, at present, you're being torn three ways. Perhaps it's time you sorted out what you really want to do with your life.'

Eliza nodded and, glancing at her watch, left the room. She knew she would have to put her problems on hold for the afternoon, as she had a group of sixth-formers to supervise.

* * *

Eliza was glad not to be in school the following day and, after helping her father in the bakery for a few hours, decided to go over to Lilac Cottage. For the time being, she'd decided not to mention the predicament she was facing at school to her family.

When she arrived at Lilac Cottage, she went upstairs and tapped on the study door. Greg opened it immediately and greeted her with a warm smile.

Gyp came rushing out of the room, barking and wagging his tail frantically, and she stooped to pat him.

'I heard the car,' Greg told her. 'I was just about to stop for a coffee break anyway.'

She followed him down to the kitchen and assembled the mugs.

'Did you enjoy your meal at the Drunken Duck?' he asked a few minutes later as they sat over coffee in the kitchen.

'Yes, thanks. How about you?'

'Certainly did. They do an excellent roast, don't they?'

She was tempted to ask him who his companion had been, but decided against it. Instead she said, 'I was wondering what you did with Gyp?'

He looked surprised. 'Oh, Kerry had him for a few hours. Her small nephew was visiting. Now, before I resume work, is there anything I can do for you?'

'No thanks. I'm just going to take another look at Eliza's room and see what can be done to brighten up my great-uncle's. Is Kerry still doing the cleaning nowadays?'

'Absolutely. She's a treasure round the house and she's quite a good cook too — supplies me with pies. Of course, you're in the cookery business yourself, aren't you?'

'Sort of. I help my father in the bakery and make and decorate cakes as a side-line. That's besides working in a school two days a week.'

He raised his eyebrows. 'Busy lady.' Getting to his feet, he said, 'I usually have a snack lunch about one o'clock. If you're still around, perhaps you'd care to join me?'

Eliza got to her feet too and followed Greg back upstairs. She spent an interesting time in her great-uncle's room, looking through his wardrobe and wondering what she ought to do about his clothes and shoes.

The furniture was very old-fashioned, as Kelvin had remarked, but it was solid and in keeping with the character of the room. She made a list of one or two items she might need to sell to make more space for her own possessions. Eliza didn't think she could live with the dark oil paintings of cows and pheasants, either. However, there were a number of Henry's personal possessions which it seemed a pity to get rid of. She would have to think about what to do with them. Great-Aunt Eliza's room wouldn't take much more than a single bed, chest of drawers, desk and an easy chair. Perhaps she could persuade her mother to come and take a look. She could certainly do with her advice.

She was sitting at Eliza's little bureau, gazing out of the window, when her mobile rang, startling her out of her reverie. It was Kelvin.

'Liza, I'm sorry, but I'm afraid I'm going to have to let you down tonight.'

'Go on,' she said, feeling an overwhelming sense of disappointment.

He cleared his throat. 'We've got a

mega problem with the play. One of our lead characters has pulled out at the eleventh hour — some family crisis — so we're going to have to audition again. On top of that, we've got to write another scene in.'

'And it's got to be tonight, has it?' she asked in a tight little voice.

He sighed. 'Liza, we've hardly any time left as it is. I'm really sorry, but I can't do anything about it. And to crown it all, I feel as if I've got a cold coming on.'

He broke off to speak to someone who'd come into the room.

'Sorry, Liza, got to go now.'

Eliza sat staring at her mobile, unable to believe what had just happened. She didn't hear Greg come into the room and jumped when he spoke.

'Sorry — didn't mean to startle you! Thought you might be ready for lunch. What's wrong? You look as though there's a gremlin in that phone!'

Eliza pulled herself together with an effort.

'Oh, it's nothing — just a friend letting me down at the last minute. We were going to a Valentine's dinner and dance tonight, but he's inundated with work and has had to cry off.'

She scrabbled about in her bag and held out the tickets.

'I suppose you wouldn't care to . . . '

'Accompany you instead? I'd be delighted.'

Eliza's cheeks flamed red. 'Oh, b-but I didn't mean . . . I thought perhaps you could use them. Actually, they're courtesy tickets. My father gets given freebies periodically from the hotels he supplies.'

There was a twinkle in Greg Holt's eyes.

'Well, I'm free this evening and you obviously are too, so . . . '

Eliza hesitated and then said on an impulse, 'Oh, why not, if we're both at a loose end.'

He smiled. 'Great! Anyway, if you're thinking of moving in and we're going to be housemates, then it would be a golden opportunity for us to get to know each other better, don't you think?'

What harm could it do? Kelvin would be taken aback when he realised she'd gone with Greg. Well, serve him right!

'OK, you're on,' she said. 'Now, about lunch. I've brought some pasties from our bakery. Shall we can warm them up in the microwave?'

'Yes, please! Wow — you're going to make some housemate!'

* * *

That evening, Eliza dressed carefully in a calf-length, sea-green dress that matched her eyes. She swept her fair hair up high and applied some make-up. Although it was to be a light-hearted affair, the venue was rather grand.

She was spared any explanations at home for the time being; her parents were out having a meal with friends, and James had gone to a Valentine's celebration of his own — a disco at the village hall with his latest girlfriend, Leanne.

Greg had arranged to pick Eliza up from the house. He was prompt and looked the part, wearing a dark suit beneath his overcoat.

The meal was superb. As they began their main course, one of the waiters came round to the tables, proffering a basket of red roses. To her acute embarrassment, Greg purchased a single red rose and presented it to her with a smile.

'I hope you'll accept it as a thank you for this evening. It beats staying in and watching TV anytime.'

For a time their conversation was on a light note, exchanging stories about their university days, but then, suddenly, she found herself telling Greg about the problems with her teaching job.

He was a good listener, and presently, he commented, 'But surely this head teacher can't just dismiss you — not nowadays?'

'Unfortunately, I'm only on a renewable contract and, in all fairness, she has offered me the full-time post. She's also said she might be able to come up with something else, like teaching assistant work, if I want to remain part-time. Unfortunately, she can't promise I'll be able to remain in Food Technology and, of course, the salary would be considerably lower.'

Greg raised his eyebrows. 'That's a tough one. Have you decided what you really want to do?'

'Not quite. It's difficult, but juggling three jobs is difficult too. Anyway, enough of me — what about you?'

He looked surprised. 'How d'you mean? I've got a job for the next few months at any rate.'

There was a pause in the conversation as the waiter whipped away their plates and brought their desserts. Eliza tackled a sumptuous chocolate concoction decorated with fresh fruit, before setting down her spoon and asking, 'What did you do before you came to work for my great-uncle?'

He chuckled. 'I worked for Henry's publisher. I was in the editorial department and Henry poached me!'

Her lovely green eyes widened. 'Really? Didn't you mind leaving the buzz of the publishing world in London to come and bury yourself away down here?'

Greg took a moment to answer, swallowing a mouthful of apricot tart, and suddenly seemed sombre.

'Let's put it this way, Eliza — sometimes a change is as good as a rest.'

She wondered what he meant by this remark, particularly when, over coffee, he advised, 'You know, if I were you, I'd think very carefully about what it is you really want to do. It seems to me you're at a crossroads in your life and, before moving on, you need to be very sure that you're making the right decision for the right reasons.'

She nodded. 'But even if I move into

Lilac Cottage, I'll have a lot of expenses, won't I? I know it won't be like having a mortgage tied round my neck, but at least the teaching brings in a reliable income, and then there's my pension to think about.'

Greg looked amused. 'You've obviously got a sensible head on your shoulders, but it would be dreadful to get to retirement age and regret not having taken the right turning at the crossroads, wouldn't it? Anyway, if I'm living under your roof as an uninvited house-guest, then the least I can do is to pay my way.'

'Oh, but . . . ' she began, embarrassed, but just then the orchestra started up.

'No buts! Let's just enjoy the rest of the evening, shall we? Would you care to dance?'

Before she could refuse, Greg took her firmly by the hand and led her onto the dance floor amongst all the other couples. He was an extremely good dancer and looked very handsome in his dark suit and white, open-necked shirt.

As he held her close she felt a little frisson trembling along her spine, and was aware of the magnetism emanating from him.

Eliza saw one or two admiring glances cast in their direction. She kept thinking that she was in the middle of some strange dream and that, presently, she would wake up and find Kelvin there instead of this mystery man.

As the dance came to an end, Greg led Eliza back to the table and she realised how much she was enjoying being in his company. After another hour, however, she told him that she ought to go because she'd got an early start at the bakery in the morning. She also didn't want Greg to feel obliged to stay until the bitter end.

They were driving through the town and had stopped at the lights when Eliza caught sight of Kelvin with his arm slung about a girl's waist. She recognised the girl as Belinda, who worked with him in the English department.

'Oh!'

The strangled sound made Greg look swiftly out of the window, just in time to spot the couple disappearing into a nightclub. The lights changed at that moment and Greg had to concentrate on his driving. He gave Eliza a moment or two to compose herself and then said matter-of-factly:

'Was that your original date?'

'How did you guess?' She felt nauseated, and choked back the tears.

'I saw him with you at the Drunken Duck the other day.'

'Right. Of course. Yes, it was. He told me he was working late tonight and that he'd got a cold coming. The girl he was with is a newly qualified teacher who joined the staff a few months back.'

'I see. You know, I've learnt from experience that sometimes it's best to give people the benefit of the doubt.'

She didn't reply, but just sat staring

miserably out of the window, wishing that she hadn't seen Kelvin and Belinda together.

Before long, Greg pulled up outside her gate.

'Thank you for a lovely evening, Eliza.' He reached across and kissed her lightly on the cheek. 'I hope we're going to be good friends.'

He sat in the car watching until she went inside, although she'd assured him that her parents would be home by now.

Eliza Ellis had made an impression on Henry Curtis and, although Greg had only just met her, he had a feeling that she was very like the lady whose name she bore.

Greg smiled to himself. No-one could have been more shocked than him when Eliza had announced she was intending to move into Lilac Cottage. He had hoped to get Henry's book finished way before she arrived on the scene. Now that he'd come to know Eliza a little better, however, he realised that she was in danger of becoming a disturbing influence in his life for quite a different reason.

3

Eliza managed to avoid Kelvin for several days without much difficulty, but then they had a staff-training day and she had to face him. He came across to her during the lunch break.

'I haven't seen you for ages. D'you fancy going out for a drink tonight?'

She knew she'd have to have it out with him sooner or later and reluctantly agreed. That evening, they drove to a pub a little way out of town. She took her apple juice over to a corner table where they could talk privately.

For a few moments they sat in silence.

'There's no easy way for me to say this, Liza,' he told her at last.

There was a tight knot in her throat as she realised her suspicions were about to become confirmed.

She swallowed hard. 'Then let me

make it easier for you, Kelvin. You're two-timing me, aren't you? And it's Belinda.'

He set down his drink so that it splashed on the table.

'How did you . . . I mean we've been discreet — so who . . . ?'

She was determined to keep calm, and not to give him the satisfaction of seeing how upset she was.

'Never mind that. At least you don't deny it. So what have you got to say for yourself?'

He ran his hands through his sandy hair. 'Belinda and I just clicked from the moment she joined the English department. She feels as passionate about drama as I do.'

'To say nothing of feeling passionate about you,' Eliza said acidly.

He had the grace to look shamefaced. 'We've been flung together, what with the Christmas show and the play — and now she's joined the drama group I belong to as well.'

'Good for her! So why's it taken you

so long to pluck up the courage to tell me you're dumping me?'

He bit his lip. 'Liza, I'm finding this really difficult because I do care about you, but our relationship has never had that special spark.'

'And you obviously think you and Belinda have got that?' she asked dully.

Kelvin nodded. 'I didn't mean to hurt you, Liza, which is why I wanted to be very sure before I spoke to you. You see, Belinda and I are on the same wavelength with so many things. She's as dedicated to the theatre as I am.'

'I've tried to be supportive, Kel. I've attended several of your rehearsals and productions,' she said stiffly.

Kelvin looked uncomfortable and fidgeted with his beer mat.

'The problem is, you wanted more from this relationship than I did. All this talk of doing up the cottage — I could see where it was leading, but I'm afraid I'm just not ready to settle down yet. I value my freedom too much for that.'

Cheeks flaming, Eliza sprang to her feet, supposing that this was when — in all good soap operas — she would throw her drink over him. Instead, she picked up her glass and slowly and deliberately drained it.

'Right. Thanks for putting me in the picture, Kelvin,' she said, with great self-control. 'Actually, I would have thought Belinda was a little young for you, but I realise she hangs on your every word. I hope you'll be very happy together.'

And with that, she swept out of the bar with as much dignity as she could muster and headed for her car.

★ ★ ★

'Is that you, Liza?' her mother called out as she entered the house. 'You're very late, dear. I've saved you some dinner. Are you ready for it?'

'Sorry, Mum, I've got a dreadful headache,' Eliza mumbled and rushed up the stairs, fighting back the tears.

Meryl prudently waited for half an hour before taking Eliza a cup of tea.

'I don't want to pry, dear, but sometimes a problem shared is a problem halved, and you haven't been yourself for a while now.'

She sat down on her daughter's bed and gently coaxed the story from her.

Eliza sniffed. 'I've been such a fool, Mum. I should have seen the warning signs. Other people must know about Kelvin and Belinda.'

'I never did think Kelvin was right for you, dear. Oh, he's a nice enough young man, but rather self-centred, and you don't seem to have a lot in common.'

'I've tried to share his interests. I went to several plays with him and supported him both in school and in his local drama group.'

'Yes, dear, I know you did,' Meryl said gently. 'The thing is, Eliza, sometimes you're a bit impulsive. You're inclined to rush into situations and relationships headlong without thinking things through.'

Eliza was indignant. 'How d'you mean?'

'Well, take this situation with Lilac Cottage. Your father and I are very worried about you wanting to live there. It's so very isolated.' Meryl's eyes widened in sudden realisation. 'Is that what brought things to a head between you and Kelvin — did you ask him to move in with you?'

Her mother had an unfortunate knack of knowing precisely what Eliza was going to do, almost before she did herself.

Eliza sighed. 'OK, I admit I thought that if Kelvin saw the cottage he might want to make our relationship more . . . more permanent. But when I realised he didn't like the idea of living in the country or leaving his mother, then I knew I'd made a mistake. And, no, I didn't actually ask him to move in.'

Meryl patted her daughter's arm. 'Well, dear, it's seems that you might have scared him off . . . And now you're talking of sharing with this Greg

— who's a completely unknown quantity. I couldn't believe it when you told me he'd taken you to that Valentine's do. You've only known him five minutes!'

Eliza sipped her tea. 'But I've already explained. It wasn't like that at all. He's a very kind person and offered to accompany me when Kelvin stood me up. Greg's a very nice guy. If only you and Dad would come over to Lilac Cottage and meet him, then I'm sure you'd view things differently.'

Meryl pursed her lips. 'Well, Eliza, you're full of surprises, aren't you? There used to be a time when there were no secrets between us.'

'Then you'd better know that I'm thinking of handing in my notice at school and leaving at Easter,' Eliza informed her mother bluntly, and explained the situation with her job.

Her mother looked disapproving. 'That's exactly what I'm talking about, Liza. There you go again — being impulsive. The money from the bakery and what you get from your cake-making business is barely going to keep you in clothes, is it? Please, dear — I'd take a long, hard look at things, if I were you. Don't be too hasty.'

★　★　★

The following morning, Eliza was carefully decorating a Christening cake when her father came to talk to her. He watched as she finished the filigree silver and pink pattern, admiring her skill.

'You're doing a great job there, Liza. Now, have you got time for a quick coffee? There's something I want to discuss with you.'

'It'll take me ten minutes to finish this, Dad, and then I'll join you.'

Eliza wondered what her father wanted to talk to her about. She added the final touches to the cake and went into his small office.

'Your mother's been telling me you've got problems at school — both with the job itself and your relationship with Kelvin,' he began, never one to beat about the bush.

Eliza nodded. 'I've decided to leave my job. And before you say anything, yes, I have thought things through. I seem to be in a bit of a rut and time's marching on.'

'Good gracious, Eliza, you're only twenty-eight!' Roy Ellis laughed. 'You wait until you're approaching retirement, like me. You know I'd love to employ you here full-time, but I'm afraid I'm not able to pay you the sort of money you'd get at the school.'

'But money isn't everything, is it Dad? I'm beginning to realise that. Anyway, I'm going to receive a small legacy from Great-Uncle Henry's estate, when everything's settled.'

'Yes, so you've said, but I imagine you'll need all of that to pour into the cottage. Managing a home is expensive, love. Have you really thought this through?'

'Yes. My mind's made up. I'm giving

in my notice on Monday and then my head will be clearer to think about my future. And to that end, there's something I need to ask you: would you object if I used these premises for, say, one extra day a week for my own cake-making business?'

'Of course not, Liza. It's doing remarkably well, isn't it?'

Eliza smiled to herself. If she had her way, it would do even better.

★ ★ ★

Nicola Bligh, the teaching assistant shared by Eliza and Donna, didn't look too surprised when Eliza told her she'd handed in her notice.

'I have to say, I saw this coming. First Donna and now you! Liza, things just won't be the same without the pair of you. I ought to be devastated — but d'you know what?' Nicola's face suddenly broke into a broad grin. 'I'm not!'

'I didn't realise you hated working with us that much,' Eliza told her, realising her friend had to be winding her up.

'It'll salve my guilty conscience. I ought to have told you before this, but I was trying to find the right moment. My mother-in-law's project has finally got off the ground and I'm thinking of joining her in her new venture, so I'll be leaving too!'

'Her project?' For a minute, Eliza looked puzzled and then her face cleared as she remembered a conversation they'd had some months back.

'Oh, you mean the tea-shop. Wow!'

'Yep, we've finally got the go ahead and hope to have it up and running by the summer. I didn't want to let you and Donna down, and now I won't have to. It's been a dream Cynthia and I have had for years, and now it's fast becoming a reality.'

Eliza stared at her friend as something suddenly registered.

'Wait a minute — didn't you tell me the property you were interested in was in Rushden?'

Nicola beamed. 'I certainly did. It's in the old post-office premises — right on your doorstep! There's an interesting church in the area, so it could be a hit with the tourist trade, because there's no other tea-shop in the vicinity. There was quite a bit of opposition from the locals initially, when Martin and my mother-in-law attended a meeting some months back — the one I couldn't get to because of parents' evening. People don't like change, do they? Anyway, it's all going to happen at last.'

Eliza folded up a stack of clean tea-towels. 'So what does that husband of yours think about it all?'

'Oh, Martin's over the moon. He couldn't be more supportive. He knows how Cynthia and I have always fancied running a tea-shop, and now he's working up in London for such long hours, he's only too happy for us to be involved in something we're really keen on. Besides, he thinks it could be a little gold mine, so we're really made up!'

Eliza perched on one of the stools, an

idea buzzing around her head.

At last she said, 'You've just given me an amazing idea. When you open your tea-shop, if you like, I could supply all the cakes and advertise my own enterprise from a little corner of the shop — sell sugar-craft equipment, and perhaps even give demonstrations.'

Nicola whistled. 'Whoa, slow down Eliza, you're way ahead of me. For a start, wouldn't your father object? Say we're taking his trade away?'

Eliza shook her head. 'I'm already making a name for myself with my cakes for special occasions, and I've wanted more time to develop that side of things. Anyway, for some reason he doesn't supply the Rushden area. Of course, perhaps you've got other ideas. I know Cynthia's an expert at scone-making and your pastry is wonderful. I don't want to muscle in.'

Nicola picked up the pile of tea-towels.

'Actually, I think it's a fantastic idea! We were going to ask you if you could have a word with your father about supplying us with some tray-bakes. We reckoned you'd be too busy yourself, but if you're offering . . . We'd never find time to do all the baking ourselves.'

'Well, you wouldn't have to look further afield for a supplier. I'd be flexible and I'd give you a discount and obviously pay you for the advertising space.'

Nicola grinned and stuck out her hand.

'You're on! Obviously, I'll have to run it past Cynthia, but I can't see her raising any objections. I can't think of anyone I'd rather do business with — so welcome on board!'

Eliza went home with a lighter heart than she'd had for a very long time. Plans were beginning to form in her mind, and she was much more positive about her future.

After a lot of thought, she decided it might be foolhardy to move straight into the cottage without at least sorting out Great-Aunt Eliza's room. On her next visit, she broached the subject with Greg as they were sitting over coffee in the kitchen.

'You know if it's just straightforward decorating I might be able to help there,' he told her. 'Kerry — who does the cleaning — has a boyfriend, Peter. He's a carpenter by trade, but he'll turn his hand to anything. His decorating isn't at all bad. Would you like me to have a word? I promise you it won't be too expensive,' he added, as he saw her doubtful expression.

'I was thinking of tackling it myself, but the paintwork's in a bad way and the ceiling's rather high,' she told him. 'OK, could you ask him to give me an estimate? Just emulsion, I think, if the paper will take it.'

'Yes, that's probably your safest option. We don't know what's underneath so it might disturb the plaster to remove the paper. I'll have a word with Peter, shall I?'

'Please — if he can arrange a time to

see me then it'll save bothering you to show him the room.'

'It's no problem. Now, what about the furniture in that room? Are you planning to keep it?'

'The bureau's very pretty, but the chaise longue's a bit too large. I'm going to have to buy a new bed and, even if I use the wardrobes in Uncle Henry's room — if I ever finish emptying them — there still won't be too much space. If this Peter's a carpenter, then perhaps he could put up a few shelves too?'

'I'm sure he could. When you've finished bagging up the clothes do you want me to ring the nearest charity shop? Or I could help you and then take them in for you.'

Eliza beamed at him. 'You're full of bright suggestions. The sooner I can clear some space, the better. How's the book going?'

Greg laughed. 'I'm sorry, but you won't be getting my space quite yet. I've hit a slow patch *and* I'm having a problem deciphering Henry's handwriting.'

She raised her eyebrows. 'Are you telling me it's in longhand?'

'Yes, some of it. Why?'

'I assumed he'd be a computer wizard. After all, he always replied to my emails. Said he enjoyed receiving them.'

She saw Greg's slightly amused expression.

'Don't tell me you sent them? That means you read everything I wrote!'

'Would that bother you ... ? Oh, I can't pretend — actually no, whenever your emails arrived I opened them for him, but I can assure you only he read them, and he always dictated what he wanted me to say. I do have standards, you know!'

She felt embarrassed. 'Yes, I'm sure you do. I'm sorry. It's just that — well, you have to admit it was an odd situation. It meant you knew a great deal more about me, when we first met, than I did about you.'

'And does that bother you?' he asked again, his expressive grey eyes meeting hers.

She considered. 'No, not really. I've got nothing to hide.' There was a pause before she continued, 'I'd like to learn more about my great-uncle's work. I suppose . . . No, that probably wouldn't . . .'

'Go on — I'm intrigued now,' he prompted.

'Perhaps it would help if I read some of his notes for you? As a teacher, I'm used to deciphering difficult handwriting, and it might speed things up.'

'So that I can finish the job more quickly?' he enquired, eyes twinkling.

Her cheeks flamed. 'No, that wasn't what I meant. You seem to be deliberately misinterpreting my words.'

He laughed. 'Don't be so prickly, Eliza Ellis. I haven't declined your offer. Now, do you want a hand to move any unnecessary furniture out of your great-aunt's room? I wouldn't be surprised if Peter jumps at the chance of the decorating. How about we take a trip into town later — to dispose of the charity bags and pick up some paint charts?'

Eliza was bemused by the pace at which things were moving, but she supposed the sooner they got it sorted out, the better.

To her surprise, they had a fun afternoon. Greg was obviously someone who didn't hang about once his mind was made up, except where the book was concerned. They deposited the clothes at a charity shop and then went off to a DIY store to collect some paint charts.

Whilst Eliza was there, she purchased a rather nice bedside lamp and a new shade for the ceiling light.

'Food, before I fade away,' Greg pleaded.

'OK, what d'you fancy? We can call in at the supermarket on the way home.'

'There's a nice little restaurant I know, not far from here.'

'Oh, but I'm hardly dressed for

eating out!' she protested.

His gaze travelled over her trim figure dressed in jeans and a pink jacket.

'You look fine to me. Come on — I owe you one for that lovely Valentine's dinner.'

Presently, when they were seated in a corner of the pleasant but not ostentatious restaurant, he remarked casually, 'Did you manage to sort things out with your friend — about the misunderstanding on Valentine's evening?'

'It was hardly a misunderstanding, but, yes, it's all done and dusted now,' she informed him dismissively. She realised that the last thing she wanted to do was spoil their meal by talking about Kelvin.

Although she'd not long known Greg, he was clearly a good listener — but she had no intention of unburdening herself on him. It was still too painful. Not only that, she didn't want him to take pity on her and think he ought to invite her out again, just because she was on her own. After all, the silver-blonde woman mightn't like it, and Eliza had just been in that situation herself.

'So let's look at these paint charts whilst we're waiting to be served. Did you have any colour schemes in mind?'

She smiled. 'Green is nice and relaxing, so perhaps I'll go for that.'

She selected two or three shades and he marked them off carefully.

'Of course, that means I'll have to sort out cushion covers and curtains, to say nothing of a new carpet. One thing seems to lead to another, doesn't it? And that room's deceiving. It's bigger than it looks.'

'I would suggest you get the decorating out of the way first, before worrying about anything else.'

Eliza enjoyed her lunch and, as they sat drinking coffee afterwards, she realised she was feeling more relaxed than she'd done for days.

She learnt a little bit about Great-Uncle Henry's passion for history, and

Greg promised to show her the biographies the elderly gentleman had written and his original manuscripts. She noticed he said nothing about the book he was currently working on, though.

The time flew past and, almost before Eliza realised it, it was the middle of the afternoon. Greg was relaxing company, but she didn't want to take advantage of his good nature. She got to her feet.

'I've so much enjoyed lunch, Greg, but I think I ought to be getting home now. I've got a cake to ice for a twenty-first birthday.'

Greg paid the bill and they strolled back to the car park. As they passed a baker's shop she found herself telling him about Nicky's enterprise and her own ideas.

To her surprise, he didn't seem impressed.

'I'm not sure Rushden is the best place for that sort of venture,' he told her bluntly.

'Why not?' she demanded, feeling deflated.

'For one thing, that empty shop used to be a very nice post-office until fairly recently. There's a lot of feeling about its closure.'

'Yes, I read about it in the local paper. But surely, now that it's too late to save it, it would be senseless to leave it standing idle, and it's perfect for what my friends have got in mind.'

'Hmm. People round here are rather set in their ways. You'll discover that when you move in. They look out for each other and may not welcome your friends or their tea-shop.'

Eliza frowned. She couldn't understand why Greg would issue such a warning. After all, their venture seemed better than the shop standing empty.

'Do I take it someone's got it earmarked for something else?' she enquired. 'I would have thought a tea-shop would be preferable to a take-away, which seems to be the trend nowadays.'

Greg was exuding disapproving vibes.

'I've said my piece — not that it's any of my affair. So, your friends have asked you to supply the cakes for this tea-shop?'

'Well, yes. It seems a good arrangement for both of us.'

She decided not to mention that it had been her suggestion.

'Anyway, there isn't a bakery in Rushden, is there?'

There was an odd expression on his face. 'Not nowadays, no. All the bread and cakes come from Millers', the local bakery, about five miles away.' Greg paused and then added, 'They have the monopoly in this area.'

'A bit of healthy competition never harmed anyone,' Eliza rejoined, and Greg shrugged. She was puzzled by his attitude, having thought he'd have been more positive.

★   ★   ★

A few days later after a busy shift at the bakery, Eliza met up with Nicola and

Martin in the local pub in Bembury.

'We were wondering if you'd like to come and take a look at the tea-shop one day soon?' Nicola said, as they sat over their drinks in a corner of the bar.

'That'd be great. There is just one slight problem, though . . . ' Eliza told them about Greg's comments.

Nicola frowned. 'Well, that just doesn't make any form of sense. It's not as if we'd be poaching any of the regular trade from Millers', is it? We're only serving cakes, scones and sandwiches to our customers to begin with. No, I can't see where he's coming from, Liza.'

'The thing is, Nicky, I'm moving into Lilac Cottage before long, so Rushden will be my village and I want to get on with the locals.'

Nicola looked taken aback. 'So, what are you saying, Liza? Surely you're not backing down just because this chap who shares your cottage makes a comment?'

'No, of course not,' Eliza said carefully. 'That's the last thing I want to do. I just need to find out more about the opposition, that's all.'

'Monopoly, my foot!' Martin exclaimed suddenly. 'No-one can make us buy from this other bakery!'

Eliza shifted on her chair. 'I'll have a word with my father. For some reason he doesn't seem to supply this area. Anyway, surely no-one can object to my sugar-craft displays? A number of people like to buy cakes and decorate them themselves nowadays, and then of course, I was hoping to get some orders for my own celebration cakes.'

'There are bound to be a few teething problems,' Martin said seriously and couldn't understand why Nicky and Eliza laughed.

'Not with my cakes, Martin!' Eliza quipped and the conversation turned to lighter topics.

Nevertheless, she had been mystified by Greg's comments. She made up her mind to suss out the other bakery and find out more about the opposition at the earliest opportunity.

'Dad, do you know of any reason why we don't get any contracts for bakery products in the Rushden area?' Eliza asked, pausing to survey the golden anniversary cake she was decorating.

Her father looked surprised by her question.

'Oh, it goes back a long way, Liza. Arthur Miller and I have a sort of gentleman's agreement, dating back from when our families parted company to work for separate bakeries. We supply the area south of Rushden and he supplies the north — which includes Rushden itself. That way we don't encroach on each other's territory. I'd have thought you'd have worked that out for yourself, Liza. It's always been like that.'

He saw his daughter's expression. 'Now what scheme are you hatching up?'

Eliza filled him in on the tea-shop idea.

'I didn't want to mention it until it was viable, but Nicola and Martin are so keen and it would be absolutely ideal. Nicola and I get on so well, and I think it's a great idea.'

Roy sank down on a nearby chair and rubbed his forehead.

'Oh, Liza, I do so wish you'd come to me first,' he said worriedly. 'I know just lately I seem to be pouring cold water on all your schemes, but I'm not at all sure it's a good idea. I really don't want to upset Arthur or he might start coming into our territory.'

'Well, I think that's ridiculous, Dad,' Eliza told him, and began working on some golden rosebuds for the cake.

'Eliza, believe you me, it's best to leave things as they are — especially with you going to live in the area. You don't want to fall out with the locals like Henry did.'

Eliza concentrated on her task. She was working to a deadline and couldn't afford to make mistakes.

'But most of the customers won't be

living in the village, will they? They'll be visitors. So how can we possibly upset them? I'll have a word with this Arthur Miller — see if we can come to some arrangement.'

Roy Ellis looked uncomfortable. Eliza had always been strong-willed and he knew that determined look.

'Eliza, I'd really rather you didn't. Just leave things alone, love.'

Eliza was puzzled by his attitude. 'I thought you'd be pleased. Originally, I was hoping to drum up some business for you. After all, Cynthia and Nicky will need to find a supplier for their bread and rolls, but now it looks like I'll have to go it alone. I take it you won't object if I make some tray-bakes using these premises, Dad?'

'Oh, do what you like, but don't say I didn't warn you,' Roy said wearily. 'There are plenty of other venues this side of Rushden, without that one. Your cake business has done pretty well without the need for going further afield. Word of mouth has done wonders, hasn't it?'

Eliza didn't reply for a moment or two, but then she looked up.

'I'm sorry, Dad, but I'm not going to let any gentlemen's agreement stand in my way. What you choose to do is up to you, but, as for me, I'm going to produce the best cakes anyone has ever tasted for that tea-shop in Rushden!'

4

Meryl Ellis agreed to take a look at Lilac Cottage over the half-term holiday. Eliza wanted to show her the chaise longue and see if there was anything else that took her mother's fancy and, of course, introduce her to Greg. Peter was going to start on the decorating towards the end of the week.

'It's such a long time since I came here, but it seems like only yesterday,' Meryl told her daughter as they walked along the garden path.

The garden was a picture that afternoon, a mass of gold and purple crocuses and yellow aconites.

'Who sees to the garden, Liza? It's very well-tended.'

'I'm not sure — perhaps Greg does it. I've had so many other things to think about just lately that I haven't got round to asking.'

Greg was in the hall waiting to greet them, Gyp standing obediently by his side. Eliza made the introductions. Greg was dressed casually in grey trousers and a green cashmere sweater, and Eliza once again realised that he was really quite good-looking.

'Kerry came to do her cleaning stint this morning, so she's also prepared tea. I thought you might like to have it in the sitting-room. I'll go and put the kettle on, shall I?'

'That'd be great,' Eliza smiled. 'Can you give us about ten minutes? I'd like to take my mother upstairs to show her Great-Aunt Eliza's room.'

Meryl followed her daughter up the winding stairs and looked about her with interest. She stood in the doorway of Aunt Eliza's room and wondered how her daughter could want to exchange her comfortable bedroom at home for this little space. The furniture had been moved out now and the carpet removed and, to her critical eyes, it did look rather uninviting.

'Wouldn't you prefer Henry's room, dear?'

Eliza shook her head, disappointed by her mother's lack of enthusiasm.

'No, I much prefer this. You wait — when it's been decorated and there's a new carpet it'll be really cosy. That's why I wanted to show you now, before the work's done. Greg's been so helpful. As I've said, he's arranged for Kerry's boyfriend to do some decorating, and he's helped me take up the old carpet.'

'Hmm,' her mother said. 'Well, if Greg gets his feet too firmly under the table you'll have difficulty getting him to move out, dear. He seems very much at home here and very unlike a lodger — more like the host when we arrived.'

Eliza stared at her mother. 'But that's what he's had to be over the past few years. He's organised so much for Great-Uncle Henry. We ought to be grateful to him for sorting everything out. After all, it's not as if he's family.'

'That's precisely what I meant, dear.

Granted, he seems very pleasant on first meeting him, but you need to make it very clear that it's your cottage and you're in charge.'

Eliza pursed her lips and, deciding it was best not to reply to this remark, led her mother back into Henry's room and over to the chaise longue.

'Pretty, isn't it? If you'd like it then I want you to have it, but if not, it can be sold and you can still have the money.'

Meryl smiled. 'That's very generous of you, dear. It's a very nice piece of furniture and, as it belonged to Eliza, I can't see that your father would object to my keeping it.'

Before Eliza could pursue this last remark, Greg called up the stairs to say that tea was ready.

The sitting-room was decorated in subtle shades of ivory, gold and green and, although it retained its country cottage atmosphere, it had obviously been refurbished to a high standard.

'What a delightful room,' Mrs Ellis remarked.

A moment or two later, Greg brought in a laden tea-tray and made to leave.

'Aren't you joining us?' Eliza asked, disappointed.

He hesitated until Meryl added her voice to the invitation.

Greg sat down and indicated the tea-pot. 'I wonder if you'd be kind enough . . . '

Meryl smiled. 'To be mother? Of course, I usually am. Do you have a family, Greg?'

'I do indeed — parents and two sisters.'

He passed a plate of scones and then skilfully changed the subject, steering it away from himself, Eliza noticed.

'So, when was the last time you came here, Mrs Ellis?'

'Oh, now let me think . . . Eliza was around four, so it must have been about twenty-four years ago.'

Eliza saw the amused look on Greg's face and looked down at her plate, wondering how old he was. In his thirties, she supposed.

Meryl sipped her tea. 'Actually, I'd have carried on visiting Henry, but my husband discouraged me from coming here. There'd been some friction many years back — after Henry sold the bakery. I tried to mend bridges, but I'm afraid it was too late.'

There was an awkward pause and then Greg gave a little smile.

'Yes, I appreciate Henry could be quite an irascible old gentleman at times.'

'He wasn't that old when I first met him but, of course, Aunt Eliza was considerably younger. Anyway, you don't want to hear all that . . . Tell me, Greg, how do you think it'll work out with you needing so much peace and quiet? I mean, if Liza comes to live here whilst you're still working on the book?'

'Mum!' Eliza protested, pink-cheeked. 'You're making it sound as if I'm some kind of noisy nuisance!'

Greg chuckled. 'I can assure you, Mrs Ellis, it'll be just fine. After all,

Eliza's out for most of the day and, even if she is around, we're not likely to get in each other's way, because I'm generally ensconced in the study or at the library for much of the day.'

'Ah, yes, the study. It sounds such an interesting room. Is there any chance of me taking a look?' Meryl asked casually, wiping her fingers on her napkin.

For the first time since Eliza had met him, she thought Greg looked slightly ruffled, but he replied pleasantly enough.

'Certainly, but perhaps you'd just give me a few moments to tidy up? When I'm working, there are books and papers everywhere so that I've got everything to hand.'

'Oh, I didn't mean to cause a problem,' Meryl said, apologetically.

'You're not,' he assured her. 'If you've finished your tea, why don't you take a look at the rest of the rooms, by which time I'll have cleared a space.'

★ ★ ★

'That was odd,' Meryl commented a few minutes later, as Eliza took her to see the dining-room.

'I don't see why. If I was in the middle of decorating a cake, I wouldn't want anyone interrupting me either,' Eliza told her.

'No, there's more to it than that. Did you notice how Greg wasn't forthcoming about the book when I asked about it just now? You don't suppose he's finished it already and he's just biding his time here, do you?'

'No, of course not. The solicitor would know. He'd have been in touch with Great-Uncle Henry's publisher. Now, come and have a look at the kitchen.

Her mother was suitably impressed, as Eliza had known she would be.

'It's quite amazing! I suppose Greg was responsible for organising all this, was he?'

'Yes, I think he probably was. Anyway, come and see the attic and then Greg should be ready.'

As they came back down the stairs again, Greg called to them and they followed him into the study which was as neat as a new pin, with no evidence of the work he was doing, apart from some files piled up on the desk. He had spread out several books for them to look at.

'Henry's published work,' he told them.

They bent to examine the volumes, all biographies of famous war heroes such as Wellington and Napoleon.

'So what are you working on now, Greg?' Meryl asked casually.

'Sorry, but I can't divulge that just at the moment,' he said quietly.

'Oh. I had no idea the literary world was so cloaked in secrecy.'

Shortly afterwards, Eliza and her mother took their leave, as it was already getting dark.

'So what's your honest opinion, Mum? Now that you've had a look at the cottage?' Eliza asked on the drive home. 'Can you see why I've fallen in love with the place?'

There was a pause before Meryl replied.

'It's certainly in much better shape than I'd imagined and I can quite see why it appeals to you, darling, but I'm afraid I've still got my reservations.'

'Oh, why?' Eliza was unable to keep the disappointment out of her voice.

'Liza, I'm just not sure that you've really thought this through. As I've already said, I'm concerned that Greg's got his feet so firmly under the table that you're not going to be able to shift him. You must admit he swans about the place as if he owns it.'

'I think you're being unfair,' Eliza told her mother sharply. 'After all, looking at it from his angle, Lilac Cottage has been his home for a number of years. Of course he's comfortable in his environment. I think we've got a lot to thank him for, as I've said before.'

'Well, you've asked for my advice and so now I'm giving it,' Meryl said curtly.

'Greg seems a nice enough young man, but he's got a decidedly secretive manner. I mean, all that business with the book he's working on — what was all that about?'

'I expect he's got his reasons. Anyway, does it really matter?' Eliza said, impatiently. 'Stop worrying, Mum. I can take care of myself and, as lodgers go, I'm sure Greg will be great.'

Meryl was still not convinced. 'Let's hope you're right. Oh, if only your father had been there to give his input. Well, if things don't work out, you can always come back home. I promise not to let your room out!'

Eliza couldn't think of anything to say to this comment and so she remained silent.

* * *

Eliza was so busy for the next few days that she didn't have any time to dwell on her family's prejudice about her decision to move into Lilac Cottage.

One of the bakery workers was ill, and so Eliza stepped in. She spent a hectic time decorating mountains of iced fancies for a pensioners' tea-dance at a local hotel, and preparing oceans of tray-bakes for the cafés and bakers' shops they supplied.

Beyond a quick phone call to accept Peter's quote and to tell him to arrange with Greg a suitable time to commence work, and another to fill Greg in with what was happening, Eliza didn't give Lilac Cottage another thought.

She went out for a meal one evening with Nicola and Donna. Over their curry, they reminisced about the good times they'd enjoyed and toasted each other for the future.

Donna was furious that Mrs Mitchell had spoken to Eliza before she'd had a chance to do so herself.

'Of course, now that Mrs M's faced with losing her entire Food Technology staff, she's suddenly being all sweetness and light,' Nicola commented. 'She's asked Eliza and me if we'd be prepared to stay on until the summer, but we've both refused.'

Eliza nodded. 'Too right — we're raring to get on with our new project.'

But now that the moment was practically upon them, they were all feeling a bit apprehensive. She had been impressed with the old post-office in the high street, but could understand why the locals had been so opposed to its closure; particularly those whose families had lived in Rushden for many generations. There was also a lot of work to be done on the building before it could be used for a tea-shop, and so it would be several months before the business took off. The future suddenly seemed rather uncertain and Eliza could only hope that her family wouldn't be proved right. It was a big step to branch out alone.

* * *

Eliza had had a particularly busy shift at the bakery. She arrived home feeling tired and sticky, and longing for a shower and her tea. Her father had gone back after his supper to do a late shift, her mother was visiting an elderly neighbour, and James was off out with his mates.

Eliza decided to eat first. She had almost finished the cottage pie her mother had left in the oven for her, when there was a knock on the door. To her surprise, Greg was standing on the doorstep.

'Oh, it's you, Greg! What can I do for you?' she asked irritably.

Undaunted by her manner, Greg smiled and waved a handful of paint charts at her. 'I was in the area and thought I'd bring these over. Pete wants to get the rest of the paint and wasn't sure which colours you'd finally decided on for the walls.'

Eliza stared at him blankly and then, remembering her manners, said reluctantly, 'Right then you'd better come in.'

Too late, she remembered the dirty crockery on the sitting-room table and snatched up the tray. Greg stood in the doorway.

'Sorry if I disturbed you. Haven't got your mobile number. You were obviously in the middle of eating your dinner.'

Eliza sighed and pushed back a strand of hair.

'Occupational hazard, eating at irregular times, I'm afraid.'

Greg surveyed her, noting the hair scraped back unbecomingly from her face, and the floury streaks on her cheeks, to say nothing of her flustered appearance.

'You're looking tired. Perhaps you'd rather I came back another time?'

'You're here now so you might as well sit down,' she said, ungraciously, and then, as she saw his expression, added, 'I'm just about to make some coffee and there's an apple crumble — would you like some?'

'That sounds good. I take it the rest of your family's out?'

She nodded. 'My father's at the

bakery, my mother's visiting a neighbour who's had an operation on her hand and needs . . . '

'A helping hand?' he suggested.

She gave a slight smile. 'You've got it in one — opening tins and things. As for my brother — well, who knows where James might be!'

Eliza went into the hall and, catching sight of herself in the mirror, attempted to tidy up. Presently, she returned with two dishes of steaming apple crumble and a jug of cream.

'I'm afraid the custard's gone a bit solid. OK, let me take a look at those paint charts.'

He was attacking his pudding with relish. 'Delicious crumble — there's a hint of something spicy.'

'Ground cloves. My mother's recipe. She used to work in the bakery, but nowadays she helps my father with the accounts and orders.'

'So you're all into baking? It's obviously a family thing. How about your brother?'

She shook her head. 'Oh, no. James is into mechanics. He jokes that too many cooks spoil the broth!'

Greg laughed. They finished their dessert in silence and Eliza began to feel more human. She realised she'd been hungry, as she'd only had a scratch lunch and that had been hours ago.

'I'll just get the coffee, and then I'll take another look at those paint charts and sort out the colour for the walls.'

Returning, she handed him a mug of coffee and studied the charts. She was still feeling tired and not in the mood for making decisions, but realised it wasn't fair to keep Pete waiting.

Seeing her deliberating, Greg got up and leant over her chair. His closeness sent a little shiver along her spine.

'If I can offer an opinion . . . How about that pale green? It's one of those you've originally marked.'

'OK. Let's go for it. Mum's offered me an off-cut of carpet from when they had the dining-room done recently, and

I think it would all tone in well.'

'Good. That's settled then.'

He scooped up the charts. 'If you've got the carpet handy I can take it back with me.'

Eliza nodded. Feeling rather light-headed, she suddenly thought about the contrast between the Valentine's dinner dance when they'd both dressed up and there had been a romantic quality to the evening, and now, when she looked washed out, with lank hair, scruffy jeans and T-shirt.

A bubble of mirth rose within her and she began to giggle helplessly. Her laughter was infectious and although Greg had no idea what had amused her, he couldn't help but join in.

After a moment or two she reached for a tissue to wipe her streaming eyes, leant back onto the sofa cushions, exhausted from both the long day and her laughter, and tried to explain.

'Well, it's always good to share a joke,' he teased. 'I suppose you told your boyfriend you were staying in to wash your hair tonight, and then I caught you on the hop.'

'I'm aware I look a mess, but there's no need to be insulting,' she told him, yawning. 'If we're going to be sharing the cottage, you'll have to get used to me coming in at all hours and looking a bit of a fright.'

'Hey — I didn't mean to hurt your feelings!' he protested, but she ignored his protestations and, closing her eyes, promptly fell asleep.

Greg gathered up the dirty dishes and tiptoed from the room.

* * *

Presently, feeling refreshed from her catnap, Eliza went into the kitchen and found that not only had Greg done the washing up but he'd tidied round too, leaving everything looking like a new pin. Her mother would be suitably impressed.

'Goodness, I'm sorry. I don't know what came over me. I just dropped off.

You shouldn't have done all that. You're a guest.'

'A bit of an unwelcome one, by all accounts,' he smiled. 'I was trying to make amends for dropping in on you unannounced.'

She grinned. 'Let's have another coffee. If the truth's known, I've been having what you might call a bad hair day!'

They both dissolved into laughter again and, as he reached for the mugs, he brushed against her, sending a little frisson shuddering along her spine. She moved away to make the coffee, realising she was feeling vulnerable. She had absolutely no intention of becoming too friendly with Gregory Holt!

★ ★ ★

'I saw Kelvin at the club last night with that new girlfriend of his,' James announced over Sunday breakfast. 'She's quite a looker, isn't she?'

'James!' his mother warned him,

seeing her daughter's face.

'What?' he asked innocently.

'When you've finished your breakfast, you can give me a hand preparing the vegetables. Your sister and I are going to church and collecting Mrs Crouch on the way, so we don't want to be late.'

'OK, but actually, I'm not in for lunch — thought I'd told you. I'm off to Leanne's.'

'Well, you didn't. I don't know how to cater some days.'

'You're not being very fair to your mother, James,' his father added from behind the newspaper.

When his wife and son had left the room, Roy put down the paper and looked across at Eliza.

'I'm sorry about you and Kelvin, Liza. I'm sure your brother doesn't mean to be so tactless. Anyway, it's probably for the best, dear.'

Eliza didn't bother to ask him what he meant, knowing that he probably still thought of her as a little girl. One day she would surprise him by doing something to make him sit up and take notice — although she wasn't sure quite what!

'Dad, I'm going over to Lilac Cottage this afternoon. Would you like to come with me?' she asked on a sudden impulse.

Her father picked up his paper again and looked at her over the top of it.

'Eliza, I don't think keeping the cottage is one of your better ideas. I'll come over to take a look when you're properly settled in and this Greg fellow has moved out.'

'Right,' Eliza said, and began to clear the table, feeling hurt and disappointed that her father seemed so set against her moving to Rushden. Perhaps he thought he could get her to change her mind by registering his disapproval. Well, she had no intention of doing so. Her father might have a stubborn streak, but she'd inherited it!

* * *

It was early March and the days were lengthening quite nicely. There were daffodils and early primroses in the garden of Lilac Cottage.

Greg was in the garden when she arrived, tidying one of the borders. He straightened up and rubbed his back as she called out to him.

'Hi. I got your answer phone message. What a glorious day.'

'I didn't expect you to be here,' she told him, liking his rather tousled look, instead of the immaculate appearance he usually presented.

'If you've got friends coming over, I can always make myself scarce,' he volunteered.

'No, I didn't mean . . . ' Why was it she always managed to say the wrong thing when he was around? She swallowed and tried again. 'Do you always do the garden?'

'When I've got time, I like to potter about. Henry used to employ someone to prune the shrubs and apple trees. Of course, now that the cottage is yours, you may have other ideas. You'll have to tell me if I'm overstepping the mark.'

'No, don't get me wrong. It works both ways, doesn't it?' she said awkwardly. 'I mean, I don't want you to think you've got to do all the things you did when my great-uncle was alive — or at least, only if you want to.'

He smiled, and she noticed how his eyes crinkled up at the corners.

'I tell you what — let's see how it goes, shall we? I think it's best if we're straight with one another from the outset, don't you?'

'Absolutely. So, if you're sure you don't mind doing the garden . . . ? Just until I've moved in and can sort things out.'

He set down his tools. 'I enjoy it. It's therapeutic. Besides, I need some exercise or I'll put on pounds. Anyway, let's go inside, shall we? There's something I want to show you.'

As they entered the kitchen, Gyp came rushing out of the utility room, barking excitedly and wagging his tail.

'He was having a snooze when I came outside — tired out after a long walk.'

There was a faint smell of chicken in the air.

'Have you had your lunch?' Eliza asked.

'Goodness, yes — so early I've forgotten about it. Chicken casserole and veg. I can look after myself, you know. What about you?'

'I can look after myself too, thank you very much . . . oh, I see what you mean. Yes, I've had lunch too, because my mother brought her neighbour back after church.'

'The one who's hurt her hand?' he enquired, and she smiled.

'That's the one. You wanted to show me something?'

'I did indeed. Hope it'll meet with your approval.'

Mystified, she followed him upstairs and into Great-Uncle Henry's old room. He pointed her towards Great-Aunt Eliza's room.

'Cover your eyes,' he commanded and, when she obediently did so, he propelled her gently through the doorway. 'Now, see what you think!'

Slowly Eliza opened her eyes and was rendered speechless. The room had been completely transformed. Peter had done an amazing job and, on the floor, was the carpet her mother had provided.

'It's beautiful! I don't know what to say. I must owe you a mint of money.'

'That's OK. I've got the bill for the decorating, but I've already settled up with Peter because I'm aware he's got a bit of a cash flow problem at present.'

'It all looks wonderful. I can't believe what a difference it's made.'

He smiled. 'As long as you're satisfied. I know you mentioned shelves, but until I was exactly sure where your bed was going, I couldn't do much about those.'

'But I didn't expect . . . You've done quite enough already. Thank you so much!' Eliza reached out and touched his arm. 'I don't want you to think that you're a servant in this house,' she told him, 'just because you were my uncle's employee.'

He laughed and patted her hand, sending a little shockwave along her arm.

'The thought never even crossed my mind. I just happen to have a few contacts so I thought you might appreciate some help.'

'Oh, that came out all wrong again, didn't it?' Eliza said, feeling embarrassed. 'I suppose I'll have to sort out some furniture now. But before you say anything, I'd really like to do that for myself.'

He inclined his head. 'I promise to leave the rest to you, but if you want a hand, just shout.'

'Thanks. Actually, my mother's going to help me with the curtains, but we didn't get round to measuring up.'

'Wait there whilst I get a tape-measure and some paper,' he commanded.

He returned shortly, carrying a pair

of steps and brandishing the measure.

The job was done in a trice and Eliza wondered how Kelvin would have reacted if she'd asked him to help. She tried to put the thought out of her mind.

'Now, how about a cup of tea?' Greg suggested. 'Unless you've got other things to do.'

'Oh, yes please. I was wondering if I could dispose of any of this furniture,' she said, looking at the rather cumbersome Victorian dressing table and enormous armchair. 'My mother's going to have the day-bed and the little needlework table from Eliza's room, but she doesn't want any of this. And then there are those very ugly pictures!' She shuddered. 'They give me the creeps!'

Greg picked up the steps. 'You should see some of the stuff that's in my room. I'll let you take a look some time, as long as you promise not to sell it straight away and leave me with nothing but a crate to sit on!'

Eliza couldn't very well tell him that she was itching to see inside his room! It was the only place she hadn't seen, apart from the cellar and one or two cupboards.

As they sat in the sitting-room, drinking tea from bone china cups and eating a delicious chocolate cake which she assumed Kerry had made, Greg looked across at her.

'You know I wouldn't be in too much of a hurry to dispose of those items you've mentioned, if I were you; particularly the oil paintings.'

'But they're hideous!' she protested.

'That might be so, but they could be valuable. At least, Henry once hinted that they were. A family heirloom, and from your side of the family too.'

She stared at him. 'Are you telling me that my family had bad taste?'

He realised that she was winding him up and grinned.

'They obviously recognised something worthwhile when they saw it. More cake?'

She shook her head and finished her mouthful.

'No thanks; that was very good. Perhaps I should consider employing Kerry in my cake-making enterprise.'

'Sorry to disappoint you. It's not Kerry's. She's got a light touch with pastry and she's a good plain cook, but she isn't into cakes and puddings, so we've always got those from Millers' bakery.'

'Oh, I see. Well, when I move in I can keep you supplied from my father's bakery and make the cakes myself,' Eliza informed him.

'I'll look forward to the cakes, but I've got a regular bread order at the general stores and I don't want to cancel it.' He rubbed his chin. 'Perhaps I could reduce it.'

'Please yourself,' she told him, rather icily. 'I can't imagine why you need to keep on the right side of the local baker, but you must have your reasons.'

His eyes flickered. 'Loyalty, Eliza. When I move on, then that will be a different matter. Now, is there anything else I can help you with?'

'No, thanks,' she told him firmly. 'The next thing I need to do is to purchase one or two pieces of furniture, and then perhaps Peter can put up the shelving.'

'Right then, if you'll excuse me, I'm off to see some friends tonight and I've got a few things to do before then.'

When he had gone, she felt irrationally disappointed. She wandered over to the window and tried to imagine what sort of life her great-aunt had lived in Lilac Cottage. Eliza hoped she'd been happy.

She sighed. Would living here be the right step? Suppose she was making a colossal mistake? It was evident that Greg had a routine of his own and, although he was always polite and hospitable, she was beginning to realise that he said very little about himself. He had made virtually no reference to his family, or to the platinum-blonde woman he had been with at the

Drunken Duck and, somehow, Eliza couldn't bring herself to ask him. It was almost as though, deep down, she didn't want to know anything about his private life.

Presently, she went upstairs to do the job she had really come here for, which was to check out the large airing cupboard on the landing. She could have asked Greg or Kerry about its contents, but thought it was something she'd like to deal with herself.

The cupboard was fairly well stocked with quantities of neatly folded sheets, pillowcases and towels. If the bedding in her great-uncle's room was anything to go by, however, it might be of a good quality but it was also desperately in need of replacing. The towels looked as if they'd seen better days too.

She had just unearthed some exquisite hand-embroidered tablecloths and tray-cloths when the front door bell rang so loudly that she nearly fell off the stool she was standing on. Greg's door shot open to reveal him in dark trousers and a crisp white shirt, cuffs still unfastened. He took the stairs two at a time and, a moment or two later, Eliza could hear the sound of muffled voices in the hall.

Peering over the banisters, she caught a glimpse of the platinum-blonde woman. Feeling guilty for spying on them, she watched Greg place an arm on the woman's shoulder and steer her into the sitting-room.

Wait a minute, Eliza told herself, it's your cottage not Greg's, and in spite of all his protestations about not wanting to invade her space, he'd done exactly that!

She stacked the linen back in the cupboard and shut the door, irritably aware that she was feeling left out of things.

A few minutes later, Greg came back upstairs.

'A friend of mine's arrived earlier than I'd expected. We're dining with other mutual friends this evening.'

'Yes, you've said,' she told him

shortly. 'I'm just about to leave anyway. I've got an early start tomorrow. Thanks for everything.'

Greg disappeared into his room again, presumably to finish dressing for his date with the glamorous mystery woman.

5

'Well, that was unexpected,' Nicola remarked, scooping up the bouquet of flowers she'd been presented with at the little farewell do the rest of the department had arranged for the three of them.

'I feel quite teary,' Eliza said, gathering up her own gifts, 'and Donna was really upset.'

'She was the only one out of the three of us that didn't really want to leave. After all, it was only because of her husband's job.'

'Yes. Oh, Nicky, do you think we've made the right decision? It's a bit of a leap into the unknown for us, isn't it?'

'Don't start getting second thoughts now! At least you've got your job in the bakery to fall back on if things don't work out. Or you could probably get another teaching post.'

Eliza shook her head, remembering Greg's words.

'No, I've come to a crossroads in my life and I'm ready for a change. The thing is, is Rushden ready for us?'

★ ★ ★

The period leading up to Easter was incredibly busy. Eliza and her father worked flat out, trying to meet all the additional orders for the weekend. She had decorated so many individual birds' nest cakes and filled them with sugar eggs that her head was spinning. The larger cakes, mainly chocolate or lemon, needed myriads of motifs ranging from rabbits to daffodils. She also iced a large Simnel cake, thoughtfully provided by her parents for the congregation of Bembury church to share on Easter Sunday.

Eliza moved into Lilac Cottage just after Easter. It was a beautiful spring day. The daffodils waved their golden heads and the magnolia tree was a mass of pink-tipped blooms.

Nicola and Martin had volunteered to lend her a hand. Eliza had decided against telling Greg, in case he thought he had to leave his work and come to help her again, but she was disappointed to find there was absolutely no sign of him that morning.

The furniture had arrived the previous week, and Eliza had arranged to be there. She was pleased with her purchases and, apart from hanging the curtains, the room was more or less ready for occupancy.

Nicola admired the cottage. 'Wow, this is quite something, Liza!'

Martin, always a quiet man, looked thoughtfully about him. Eliza was aware he was absorbing everything.

'It's in pretty good shape considering how old it is,' he said at length. 'This fellow you're sharing with is to be commended.'

'I hope he's not too pedantic. I'm not exactly the tidiest of individuals and I like a home to look like a home — not something modelled on the Ideal Homes' Exhibition.'

'But Liza, you're an absolute fanatic about keeping the Food Technology room sparkling.'

She nodded. 'I can't work in chaos and I'm a stickler for hygiene; health and safety regulations!'

'There you are, then!'

Martin looked up from reading the newspaper that Greg had left on the kitchen table. 'So where is this fellow then?'

Eliza shrugged. 'I've absolutely no idea — probably out walking Gyp. Anyway, folks, do you want coffee before or after the curtain-hanging ceremony?'

'Both!' they shouted in unison and, laughingly, took their mugs of instant coffee upstairs and into Great-Uncle Henry's room.

'What dreadful paintings!' Nicola said and, as this echoed Eliza's sentiments entirely, Martin volunteered to remove them and replace them with a couple of Monet prints Eliza had found stashed on top of the wardrobe.

Peter had made a good job of the shelves and, presently, while Martin hung the curtains, Eliza and Nicola began to unpack some of Eliza's books.

After a hectic morning they sat enjoying a picnic lunch in the kitchen. Eliza assured them that she'd manage the rest, now that her room had been set to rights. It was around two o'clock when they heard Gyp barking, and a moment or two later Greg put in an appearance.

After Eliza had made the introductions, Martin said, 'You know I've got a feeling we've met before . . . Could it have been at that meeting in the village hall, a few months back? When people were so opposed to us wanting to turn the old post-office into a tea-shop?'

'It might well have been,' Greg replied smoothly. 'A good many of Rushden's inhabitants were there, still smarting after losing the battle to retain the post-office.'

Turning to Eliza he said, 'If you'd told me you were planning to move in today, I'd have arranged to be around. I had some business to attend to in town, but I could have postponed it. Anyway, I must get back to the computer. Nice meeting you all.'

And he disappeared up the stairs, Gyp close behind him.

'Perhaps I ought to have let Greg know exactly which day I'd be moving in,' Eliza said awkwardly, aware that she'd previously criticised him for turning up unannounced at her parents' house.

'It's your cottage, Eliza. You don't have to keep Greg informed of your movements,' Nicola told her. 'Anyway, why ever did he go to that meeting? Did he stand up and say anything, Martin?'

'Come on, Nicky — you honestly can't expect me to remember who said what, that far back.'

'I wonder why he went,' Eliza mused.

'To show solidarity, because he felt strongly about the closure of the village post-office, I suppose,' Nicola suggested. 'Knowing it couldn't be saved, like any interested local resident, he decided to see what was happening.'

'Actually, there could be any number of reasons,' Martin told them.

Eliza snapped her fingers. 'Yes, it was probably before Great-Uncle Henry died, so Greg would have wanted to feed everything back to him, wouldn't he?'

She was mystified, however, as to why Greg would want to involve himself in village affairs if he'd no intention of remaining in the area.

Martin had wandered into the garden and they followed him outside. He was examining a clump of purple pasque flowers.

'Does this wonder boy do the garden as well as everything else?'

Eliza repeated what Greg had said about his role at the cottage.

Martin stroked his chin. 'I think you're going to find yourself with a sitting tenant,' he commented.

'That's what my family think, but I'm sure you'll all be proved wrong, it's my belief that when Greg's finished Henry's book, he'll be off and away.'

'But you have to admit it's a funny sort of set-up, Liza,' Nicola remarked. 'Are you quite certain you want to stay here?'

'What's wrong with everyone?' Eliza demanded crossly. 'I get the opportunity to branch out on my own and do something I'm really keen to do, but people seem determined to see nothing but obstacles in my way.'

Nicola was somewhat taken aback at her friend's strong reaction.

'Sorry Liza, forget what I said. And remember, if you need anything then just pick up the phone. We're only a short distance away.'

After they had gone, Eliza suddenly felt a bit flat. She decided to go back upstairs and sort out the rest of her things. On an impulse, as she reached the landing, she knocked on the study door. There were things she needed to discuss with Greg.

'Come in. It's open!' Greg called out. He was sitting in front of a pile of papers, a frown on his face and a pair of spectacles perched on the end of his nose.

'Sorry! You're obviously busy. I'll catch you later.'

'No, it's fine,' he assured her. 'Is there a problem?'

'Not exactly. It's just that now I've moved in, I think that there are a few things we need to discuss, don't you?'

Greg removed his glasses and looked at Eliza thoughtfully.

'And what might they be?'

'We-ell.' She paused, suddenly feeling a bit foolish, and then she took a deep breath. 'Actually, there are quite a few things. I mean we need to think about shelf space in the kitchen for our own food — unless, of course, we have a kitty and . . . '

'Good gracious! That sounds like university days all over again!' Greg exclaimed, raising his eyebrows. 'I'm sure we can come to some civilised arrangement, but if you don't mind, I do need to get on now. How about I take you out for dinner tonight — as a welcome to Lilac Cottage? Say sevenish?'

He saw her hesitate and added, 'Unless, of course, you've made other arrangements with your, er . . . friend?'

She shook her head, wondering why she didn't tell him straight out that she and Kelvin were no longer an item. Instead she asked, 'And what about you?'

He looked surprised. 'Oh, I haven't any other plans for tonight.'

'So, does your friend live in the area?' she couldn't resist asking.

Greg frowned. 'Who? Oh, you must mean Tash — Natasha Milton,' he said seeing her enquiring glance. 'No, she lives in London. Actually, I ought to have introduced you. She was Henry's editor.'

'I see,' she said, although she didn't really see at all. Was this Natasha person Greg's girlfriend, or what?

She was still standing by his desk when Greg looked rather pointedly at his watch.

'Look, I don't wish to appear rude but I'm on a really difficult section — so if you wouldn't mind . . . ? I'll see you later.'

'I did offer to help you,' Eliza reminded him.

'And I appreciate that but, for the moment, Tash is going to pop in periodically so that we can discuss progress and iron out any problems,' he told her and turned back to the manuscript in front of him.

This wasn't how she'd imagined it, she thought crossly. Surely he could have let her lend a hand with what he was doing? Going back along the corridor, she unpacked another box — mainly sheets and towels she'd had when she was at university — and stowed them away in the capacious airing cupboard. She'd already made a pile of Henry's stuff to send to the next jumble sale.

Presently, she donned an anorak, deciding that a walk would do her good. Rushden was an attractive village with a handful of shops, a church, a village hall and a pub.

The general store was amazing. It was stocked from floor to ceiling with just about anything one could want. She had a quick look round and selected a few basic groceries. Her main reason for coming in, however, had been to suss out the bakery products and see if they really did match up to hers, and also to ask the shopkeeper if she could leave a few cards advertising her celebration cakes.

The woman seemed friendly at first. She rang up Eliza's purchases and then when she'd taken her money said, 'So you've moved into the village, you say?'

'Yes. I'm living in Lilac Cottage. It used to belong to an elderly gentleman called Henry Curtis.'

The woman's expression changed. 'Right — and you would be . . . ?'

'Eliza Ellis. Henry Curtis was my great-uncle by marriage. He left me the cottage and he . . . '

She trailed off, seeing the woman's hostile look.

'Did you say Ellis? Do I take it you're related to the people who used to own the Rushden bakery?'

'Well, yes — my family are still in the trade, over in Bembury. Actually, that's the other reason I'm here today. I wondered if I could leave you some of my cards. You see I make and decorate cakes for special occasions and . . . '

The woman pursed her lips. 'We already buy our cakes from Millers', Miss Ellis.'

Undaunted, Eliza leant on the counter. 'Yes, I know, but this isn't the same thing at all. Look, I don't want to encroach on anyone's territory, but I would have thought a little healthy competition mightn't come amiss.'

She peered at the small display of cakes and pastries.

'You don't seem to have a very big selection here.'

'Well, what d'you expect? It's almost closing time,' the woman snapped. 'Millers' offer a good range of bakery products. People come from miles around — so thanks, but no thanks.'

Feeling a little dispirited, Eliza picked up her shopping and left the store. She supposed she ought to have heeded Greg's warning. After all, he had been living in Rushden for quite some time. She walked along to the old post-office and peered through the window.

'Hallo, Eliza! Did you like the shelves?' Peter, Kerry's boyfriend, suddenly appeared from inside the butcher's and came to stand beside her.

'Yes, wonderful, thanks Peter. I'm sorry I haven't had the chance to catch up with you. I only moved in today.'

'Right — well, if you need anything else doing . . . ' He hesitated and then added, 'Kerry's a bit worried that now you're moving in, you won't want her to work for you.'

Eliza clapped her hand to her mouth. 'Goodness, I ought to have had a word with her. Look, let's leave things as they are for the time being, shall we?'

After all, if Greg was sharing the cottage, he could hardly expect to have everything for free.

'Some friends of mine are moving into these premises soon. They're going to turn it into a tea-shop. Perhaps there'll be some work for you.'

Peter looked awkward. 'Yes, I've heard about that. There's a lot of prejudice in this village. No-one wanted the old post-office to close and, now that it has, they're a bit sniffy about what it's going to become. It's a dreadful inconvenience for elderly folk to have to get into the town for their pensions and the like. We really need something that'll benefit the whole community.'

Eliza bit her lip, realising it was useless to pursue her own cake-making enterprise at this moment.

'Well, it's quite a large shop so

perhaps my friends could stock a few knick-knacks to make it into more of a tourist attraction.'

Peter shook his head. 'But, don't you see, that's just what we don't want. The worry is that a tea-shop will increase the number of visitors and bring too much traffic through the village.'

He had given Eliza a lot to think about as she walked briskly back to Lilac Cottage. She wished Nicola had been free to have attended that meeting some months back. Martin had made light of the objections, and had been a bit vague as to what they had actually been about, but it would be dreadful if they encountered real resistance from the villagers.

★　★　★

Eliza was undecided what to wear for dinner with Greg. She met him returning from a walk with Gyp. He seemed to have shaken off his sombre mood.

144

'Oh, smart casual — just be yourself,' he told her.

Eliza was in a quandary, wondering what exactly he meant by *smart casual*. In the end, she teamed a pair of black trousers with a pretty, mulberry-coloured tunic top and found some silver earrings and a matching necklace amongst her few jewellery items.

Greg's idea of *smart casual* turned out to be a beautifully-tailored green jacket, lighter green trousers and a stripy, open-necked shirt. As they sat facing each other across the table in the select restaurant he had chosen, he smiled at her.

'OK, fire away. What exactly did you want to sort out?'

Eliza swallowed, determined to keep control of the situation.

'So, what about meal times for a start? Do you want to join me or to eat on your own?'

He surveyed her solemnly. 'Do you mean like that play by Terence Rattigan — *Separate Tables*?'

She looked at him uncertainly, wondering if he was being serious.

The waiter arrived with the wine list and, after consulting with her, Greg ordered half a bottle of Chardonnay.

'OK,' he said again, as they began their starters. 'How would it be if we said dinner together when we're both around, taking it in turns for the cooking, and breakfast — again when we're both free — at around eight o'clock. We both work unsocial hours. I might work well into the night on occasion and, obviously, you'll have incredibly early starts at times, too. Let's have some sort of system, so that we each know when the other's in . . . Now, what's next?'

She opened her mouth to tell him that she'd prefer to be the one setting the rules, but closed it again, as she realised he'd actually made a perfectly reasonable suggestion.

After a moment, she said, 'Right, so now that we've sorted that one out, what are we to do about getting the

146

food — oh, and Kerry?'

He raised his eyebrows enquiringly. 'Kerry? How d'you mean?'

She coloured slightly. 'Well, normally I'd do the cleaning myself, but as Kerry is . . . '

'Already working for me? Oh, you mean payment. That's all right. I'll continue to pay her as before. I've told you, I don't expect to stay on without paying my share, but I'm afraid I'm not offering rent, as that's part of my contract.'

He was very direct and she didn't wish to appear money-grabbing.

'No, I didn't mean you to. Look, let's start again. I don't know exactly what financial arrangements were made by my great-uncle, regarding your expenses.'

She felt even more naïve because it hadn't occurred to her to discuss this with the solicitor, although surely he ought to have filled her in more clearly? It all seemed a bit vague.

Greg seemed to follow her train of thought.

'I take it you didn't discuss it with Neil Hughes? Right, let me explain. Henry stated in his will that I can live here, rent free, until I've finished the work he'd instructed me to do. For this, I'm to be paid a generous salary, which includes an allowance towards my meals and general expenses.'

'I see,' Eliza said, as she finished her starter. 'So what do you want to do about our food?'

'Food, glorious food!' Greg exclaimed loudly, sending the waitress, who had appeared to remove their dishes, scurrying off into the kitchen. When she returned a few minutes later with their main course, Greg said solemnly, 'Thank you so much. I'm absolutely ravenous.'

Eliza could hardly contain her mirth until the poor woman had gone.

'What?' Greg asked innocently, just as her brother might have done.

'That poor woman thought you were fed up with waiting for your food.'

He chuckled and began to tackle his steak with relish.

'OK. So tell me what you've got in mind regarding meals, shopping and this so called kitty.'

They worked something out to their mutual satisfaction as they ate their meal. It was beautifully cooked and, until that moment, Eliza hadn't realised just how hungry she was.

'Next item?' Greg demanded presently.

She considered. 'Well, I suppose we could sort out anything else as and when it crops up. I'll try to respect your working routine if you'll respect mine.'

There was a glint in his eyes. 'Hmm, does that mean you'll be cake-making from Lilac Cottage?'

Eliza shook her head. 'Not at present, no. Although it's a lovely kitchen, there are a number of hygiene rules that have to be observed. For instance, Gyp — lovely animal that he is — is often in the kitchen, isn't he?'

Greg frowned. 'You want me to keep him out? That might prove difficult at times.'

She concentrated on her meal. The lamb noisettes were succulent and melted in her mouth. She realised that Greg had been living at the cottage for some time and was likely to find it difficult to change his habits. Be that as it may, she didn't see why she had to fit in with him rather than the other way round.

'I'm not asking you to keep Gyp out of the kitchen entirely and, for the present, I'll continue to make cakes at the bakery. However, when I'm cooking the meal, I wouldn't expect to have a dog under my feet.'

He nodded. 'Point taken — let's see how we muddle along together then, shall we? We can have another chat in a week or so. There are bound to be minor irritations on both sides, don't you think?'

'It must have come as quite a shock to you when you realised I intended to live in Lilac Cottage whilst you were still in residence,' she said, meeting his gaze levelly.

'Goodness, you make me sound like royalty.' He speared some peas on his fork. 'It must have been an even greater shock when you realised you'd got an unexpected lodger!'

He ate the peas and then said, 'Anyway, seems like we're stuck with each other for the time being, so we might as well make the best of it!'

Eliza opened her mouth to retort, and then thought better of it and popped a piece of mushroom in, instead.

Fortunately, the soft background music prevented them from eating in complete silence for the next few minutes. Presently, Greg set down his knife and fork with a sigh of satisfaction.

'That was very welcome. How did you get on in the village stores, by the way?'

Startled, Eliza stared at him. 'How did you know?'

'It didn't take too much working out. You were carrying a bag with their logo on it and you were on foot. I saw you from the window!'

She sighed. 'It's a nice shop, although the prices are rather steep. Oh, and you might as well know, you were quite right — the assistant wasn't at all interested in my cake-making enterprise. Which is a pity, because what they had on show looked decidedly uninteresting, to say nothing of being curled up at the edges.'

Greg sipped his wine. 'I think you're being a tad unfair, Eliza. The bakery products are usually very good, and you must remember that the shopkeeper has to keep in with her regular supplier. As far as she's concerned, you're a totally unknown quantity.'

Eliza coloured. 'Not totally. It would seem some people have heard of my family. Perhaps you ought to fill me in as to why there's so much prejudice around here.'

He shrugged. 'Perhaps you ought to leave things be and just concentrate on selling your cakes to your usual market.'

'Thanks for the advice; I'll bear it in mind,' she told him, feeling he was being patronising. 'I've got plenty of other outlets — but I don't intend to give up without a struggle.'

The waitress brought their desserts and for a few moments Eliza concentrated on her lemon meringue, which was delicious.

'You know, I think this arrangement could work quite well,' Greg commented suddenly. 'We don't need to cross each other's paths that often and, when we do, I'm sure we can be civilised. The only stipulation I must make is that, when I'm working, I don't like to be disturbed too often.'

'Ditto,' she said icily. 'There's a surprising amount of work attached to my job — designs, costing, and so on. How's the book coming on, by the way?'

He smiled and dipped a spoon into his ginger pudding before replying.

'You haven't asked me that for at least a week. I've recently emailed a chapter to Tash, and she'll need to see me soon because she's got a few queries. As I've explained, it's a slow process. Sorry to disappoint you, but I'll be around for a while yet, so we're just going to have to make the best of it, aren't we? Now are you ready for coffee?'

* * *

That night in her great-aunt Eliza's little room, Eliza tried to sleep, but thoughts kept whirling round in her head. She'd enjoyed the meal with Greg, but was disappointed that he felt that they should, for the most part, go their separate ways.

Eliza suddenly felt extremely alone and wondered if she'd been wise to move into Lilac Cottage whilst he was still around.

As she lay there, sleep evading her, she heard a distinct tapping sound on the window and shot up in bed, straining her ears to listen. It came

154

again, sounding eerily like someone knocking against the window. She tried to tell herself that that was ridiculous. It wasn't as if she was on the ground floor.

A shiver ran down her spine as the sound came once more and, this time, she grabbed her dressing-gown, rushed along the corridor and hammered on Greg's door. He opened it swiftly, tying the belt of his own dressing-gown about him.

'What's wrong? You look as if you've seen a ghost.'

'There's someone outside my window,' she said shakily.

'Stay there,' he commanded and, picking up a heavy door stop, went to take a look whilst she hovered in the entrance.

'It's OK,' he told her a few minutes later. 'Come over here and take a look.'

He caught her arm and drew her reluctantly towards the window. She looked out gingerly and, to her relief, saw the branch of a tree brushing the window in the wind.

She felt foolish, but Greg put a reassuring arm about her shoulder.

'Come on, you've had a busy day, and it's not surprising you're finding it hard to sleep in a strange environment. This old cottage has its own particular noises. The wind whistles down the chimney, and there are creaks, and sometimes the pipes make dreadful noises too. Anyway, rest assured Gyp would have barked if anyone had been around. He's a pretty good guard dog. Now, how about some hot chocolate? That's what I used to get for Henry when he couldn't sleep.'

The arm about her shoulder was comforting and she could feel the heat emanating from his body through her thin night attire. Emotions stirred within her.

Looking up she met his gaze and saw from his expression that he was aware of the chemistry too.

As they sat at the kitchen table, Eliza began to relax. She realised what a nice person Greg was and decided she'd like to get to know him better.

This time when she went back to her room she slept soundly and awoke feeling refreshed and ready to face the new day. To her disappointment, there was no sign of Greg, so she breakfasted alone before driving over to Bembury.

★   ★   ★

Eliza loved the variety of the work at the bakery. First she decorated a Thomas the Tank Engine cake for a four-year-old's birthday party, and then she tackled a complicated design on a cake for a golden wedding anniversary celebration, with gold filigree and tiny golden bells and rosebuds. To finish, she piped the names of the happy couple in the centre. After this, she began work on a christening cake with blue and silver tracery, topped with a baby in a crib.

Eliza joined her father in the office for a quick lunch break and, in between mouthfuls of ham and cheese rolls, answered his questions about the previous day.

'So, did you settle in all right?' Roy enquired.

She filled him in briefly with the previous day's happenings, omitting the part about her scare in the early hours.

'Greg's been more than helpful. He took me out for a meal last night to welcome me to Lilac Cottage.'

Roy looked sceptical. 'I see. Well he obviously wants to make a good impression, hoping you'll allow him to stay on.'

'Dad! I wish you'd meet him, and then you wouldn't be so suspicious. He's really very nice when you get to know him.'

Her father frowned. 'So you keep telling me. What about this book — has he almost finished? What's it all about, anyway?'

'I'm not sure,' Eliza said, wishing she knew the answer to that one herself.

'Hmm, well, you need to do your

homework, my girl. I won't be the only one asking that particular question, I'm sure.'

Eliza got up to make some coffee. 'I keep hoping you'll come over to the cottage. You know you'd be more than welcome.'

Roy helped himself to another roll. 'I will, just as soon as I can make the time, although it's a little awkward.'

Eliza handed him his coffee. 'How is it awkward? What d'you mean, Dad?'

'Oh, nothing you need concern your head about, Liza. Forget I spoke.'

Before she had a chance to question her dad further, one of their workers popped her head round the door to tell him a delivery man had arrived and, by the time Roy returned, the moment was gone.

That evening, Eliza went into the office to have a quick word with her mother before returning to Lilac Cottage. Mrs Ellis looked up with a smile.

'I've missed you so much, Liza. When are you coming to supper?'

Eliza laughed. 'When I've run out of food!'

She perched on a chair. 'Mum, I'm a bit mystified. I've heard Dad talk about Arthur Miller, and he sounds a reasonable sort of man to me, so I really don't understand why he would object to me advertising my cake-making business in Rushden. Whenever I mention it, people tell me it's a bad idea.'

Her mother looked uncomfortable. 'It's complicated, dear. It all stems back to when the bakery was in Rushden.'

'But we're going back years, to Great-Aunt Eliza's time, aren't we?' Eliza was determined to get to the bottom of things. 'What can have happened all that time ago that still has any relevance now? Surely people would like a choice when it comes to being able to order a wedding or birthday cake. I mean, let's face it, plenty would go to the nearest supermarket.'

'As I've already said, it's complicated, dear.' Her mother sighed again, before going on, 'Oh, I might as well tell you before someone else does. Henry sold the bakery, just a short while after Eliza died. Your uncle Fred was in charge and your father was assistant manager. Henry came into the office one day and coolly announced that he'd sold the bakery lock, stock and barrel to someone who wanted to build a house on the site. There was no warning — the staff just lost their livelihoods overnight.

'Well, your Uncle Fred had an enormous row with Henry and stormed out of the building. As you know, Fred went to Canada, but your father was left to face the music — all those poor employees. Afterwards, he told Henry he would never set foot in Lilac Cottage again.

'So, you see, dear, it's all a matter of principles and pride. Eventually, Arthur Miller and his family set up the bakery on one side of Rushden, and your father joined his friend here in Bembury, until the opportunity arose for him to buy him out.'

Meryl paused and then added, 'The problem is that people have long memories, and they remember the hard times before Miller's bakery was established.'

Eliza said heatedly, 'Well, it was hardly Dad's fault, or Uncle Fred's and, anyway, Great-Uncle Henry wasn't even an Ellis.'

Meryl smiled wryly. 'No dear, but people felt that your father and Uncle Fred should have made a firmer stand.'

Eliza picked up some paperclips from the carpet.

'Well, times have moved on and it's all in the past. It seems as if both my father and Arthur Miller have managed to survive and rebuild their lives and, no doubt, most of the others have too.'

Meryl shook her head. 'That's not really the point, Liza. Ellis's bakery ought to have still been around in Rushden today. It was founded in Victorian times and was to have been Fred's inheritance, and then it would have stayed in the family.'

162

Eliza wasn't so sure. 'How do you make that out? Quite apart from the fact that Uncle Fred and his family live in Canada, I don't think either Paul or Jacky have ever shown much interest in running a bakery and neither has James — so that only leaves . . . '

'You, Eliza,' her mother finished for her. 'You have the aptitude and would have carried on the family tradition in Rushden.'

Eliza caught her breath. 'So that's why Dad said Great-Uncle Henry left me the cottage to salve his conscience.'

Meryl had certainly given her daughter plenty of food for thought.

★   ★   ★

On the way home she stopped off at the supermarket and decided they'd have to make do with something quick and easy for supper that evening — like a stir fry. She was preparing the vegetables when Greg came into the kitchen.

'Sorry, I meant to tell you — I'm out

to supper tonight. Have you had a good day?'

Eliza nodded, feeling a sharp pang of disappointment that he wasn't going to be there.

'It's business mixed with pleasure, actually,' he told her, as if to soften the blow. 'Tash is visiting her relations and I've been invited to dinner.'

He was going out of the door when he added, 'Actually, my friends live in the Old Bakery that once belonged to your family. I'll arrange to take you over there some time. I expect you'd find it interesting — not that there's much left of the original building now. See you at breakfast!'

Eliza ate a solitary meal, and then settled down to work out some designs for a diamond wedding cake. She was watching a film on TV when she heard the front door opening and the sound of voices. A few minutes later, Greg knocked on the sitting-room door.

'I've brought Natasha back so that we can run through the next chapter of

Henry's book. Sometimes it's easier than continually emailing. See you in the morning.'

Before Eliza could reply he had gone. She heard the sound of laughter as they made their way up the stairs to the study. She had been in bed for quite some time when she heard the crunch of tyres on gravel and realised Greg was running Natasha back to the Old Bakery.

They obviously had a good relationship and she wondered if it was just work, although why ever should it matter to her? After all, Greg's private life was none of her business. She fell asleep before he returned, to dream that he was showing her great-uncle Henry's latest book which was about cake decoration!

6

Greg obviously didn't need much sleep. By the time Eliza had come down for breakfast the following morning, he'd already taken Gyp for a walk and laid the table.

'Didn't you tell me you've got some free time this morning?' he asked, as they sat over scrambled eggs and coffee.

Eliza reached for another slice of toast. 'Yes, a few hours. I'm going into the bakery this afternoon to finish decorating a couple of cakes ready for the weekend. I take time off as and when I can.'

Greg passed her the butter. 'Rather like myself. It's a lovely April morning and I fancy taking a bit of time out too . . . Do you want to join me?'

'What had you got in mind?' she asked casually, not wishing to appear too eager.

'I rather wanted to follow up on what I mentioned last night and take you to see my friends at the Old Bakery.'

He'd taken her unawares. 'Oh, I don't know — perhaps that isn't such a good idea,' she said doubtfully.

Greg looked surprised. 'Why ever not? Rowland Rawlings — the elderly gentleman who lives there now — was a friend of Henry's and I thought you'd be keen to learn a bit more about your great-aunt from him.'

'But would I be welcome?'

Greg smiled. 'Of course! Don't look so worried. I promise these particular natives are friendly — even if some of the others round here haven't proven to be. You've just got to show everyone that you're like your great-aunt: determined to succeed.'

Eliza wasn't convinced but realised that if she backed down now, Greg probably wouldn't ask her to accompany him again.

* * *

The Old Bakery was practically hidden behind a high laurel hedge. Eliza looked about her with interest. The gardens were beautifully tended with a mass of spring flowers and flowering shrubs. The house of mellow brick gave no clue as to its past.

To Eliza's dismay the door was flung open by Natasha, looking elegant in a white trouser suit, and with a smile that was entirely for Greg.

'Saw you coming. Come along in.'

The elderly gentleman in the recliner chair looked up with a smile as they entered the room.

'Hallo Greg, and I take it this young lady is Eliza Ellis? My goodness, you're so like your great-aunt, there's no mistaking you!'

Eliza warmed to Rowland Rawlings immediately, and perched on the chair beside him, aware, as she did so that Natasha was deep in conversation with Greg.

After a moment or two, a slim, attractive older lady entered the room

168

with a tray of coffee.

Rowland beamed. 'This is my wife, Phoebe. Has Greg explained that Tash here is her cousin? Tash often stays with us because her own folk live abroad.'

'Rowland, I don't suppose Eliza wants my life history. She's more interested in finding out about Henry's wife — the other Eliza,' Natasha told him and handed round the coffee.

'So, what do you want to know?' the elderly gentleman demanded.

'Well, er — anything of interest, I suppose,' Eliza floundered.

Natasha looked amused and turned away to talk to her cousin and Greg.

'Eliza Curtis was a very attractive young woman, as you are yourself, my dear. That was when I first knew her.' Rowland sighed. 'As time went on, unfortunately, she became so ill that she looked wan. Henry did everything he could but sadly, she just slipped away.'

'She was a lot younger than her husband, wasn't she?'

'Yes, indeed she was. Of course,

Phoebe's a lot younger than I am. She came to be my housekeeper, after my first wife died, and ended up marrying me!'

'So, how come you're living here?' Eliza asked curiously. 'Did you buy the house from my Uncle Henry?'

There was a pause and then Rowland said incredulously, 'No! My goodness, you really don't know much about your family history, do you? Anyway, first things first. What made you decide to return to Rushden when the rest of your family have stayed away all these years?'

'I inherited Lilac Cottage,' Eliza said, simply.

Rowland studied her thoughtfully.

'Yes, I am aware of that. But, to be perfectly frank, we thought you'd sell it.'

'Why?' Eliza asked, and he laughed.

'That's just the sort of reply your great-aunt would have given. You must have your reasons for coming to Rushden. Was it just the attraction of living in the cottage?'

'No, although it was a golden opportunity to branch out on my own. Getting a foothold on the property ladder isn't easy these days.'

'Bet you didn't reckon on having a lodger,' Rowland chuckled.

'I don't suppose Greg was too smitten with the idea either,' she said, tartly.

'Oh, I think we're going to muddle along OK together, don't you, Eliza?' Greg asked softly, and winked at her.

The colour tinged Eliza's cheeks, as she realised everyone was looking at her.

'Fortunately, the cottage is large enough for us both to have our own space. It's not as if it's going to be forever,' she said, not meeting Greg's amused gaze.

Natasha adeptly changed the subject and began telling Greg about some mutual friends who had just got engaged.

Watching the young woman, who was

sophisticated and well dressed, Eliza realised that they were poles apart. Natasha had an easy rapport with Greg and their relationship obviously went beyond that of work colleagues. Eliza decided there was something about Natasha Milton that she did not like.

After a short while, Natasha glanced at the clock on the mantelpiece.

'Goodness, is that the time! I must catch the next London train — got a million and one things to do at the office and one of our top authors is coming to see me at four. Greg, could you be a darling and drive me to the station?'

But Greg was already on his feet.

'I'll be back shortly,' he told Eliza.

Phoebe followed them out into the hall, leaving Eliza alone with Rowland. He leant towards her in a conspiratorial fashion, brown eyes twinkling.

'It's our tenth wedding anniversary at the end of the month. Greg tells me you make cakes for special occasions. I wonder — would you make us a cake?'

'I'd be delighted,' Eliza informed him, and then something occurred to her. 'But, wouldn't Miller's bakery be a bit put out?'

Rowland frowned. 'Why on earth should they be? I can buy my cakes from whoever I choose. I could go to *Harrods*, if I so wished. As it happens, Greg's offered to give us the cake as an anniversary present, and he's told us you'll do us proud.'

Eliza's thoughts were racing as she promised to drop by with some designs for the cake in a few days' time.

Shortly afterwards, Phoebe Rawlings came back into the sitting-room.

'Those two don't get to see nearly enough of each other these days. I never did understand why Greg agreed to bury himself down here.'

Rowland Rawlings gave his wife a sharp glance.

'He no doubt had his reasons, my dear. Anyway, there's nothing to prevent him from going up to London from time to time, now that Henry's no longer with us, is there?'

'Well, he won't be staying in Rushden forever, I suppose. Just until he's finished whatever it is he's doing. I'm sure he'll get a job back at the publisher's . . . Now, Eliza, would you like to take a look at the garden? Greg says you're keen to see what's left of the bakery.'

Phoebe whisked Eliza off to see the only remaining part of the Old Bakery.

'We use it as a workshop now. Not much to see, I'm afraid. Most of it was knocked down to make room for the house.'

Eliza found it a strange experience, standing where her grandparents had once stood. Phoebe pointed out part of the wall that had been retained for a garage, and where her grandparents' cottage had once been situated.

'Part of the garden's still more or less as it would have been in those days. It's a real old-fashioned country garden. Come and have a look.'

It was charming, complete with apple

and pear trees, and an old sundial.

'Rowland promised the previous owners he'd endeavour to keep this part of the garden more or less as it was. He's inclined to be a bit sentimental.'

Before Eliza could ask any questions, Greg appeared on the terrace and after a few more minutes they departed.

As they drove back to Lilac Cottage, Eliza said, 'It was kind of you to offer to provide the cake for the Rawlings' wedding anniversary, Greg.'

'Oh, good, Rowland asked you, did he?'

'Yes, but I would like to make it clear that I'm quite capable of finding my own customers. I don't want you to think you've got to sponsor me. I'm not a charity case.'

'I didn't think for one moment that you were,' he said smoothly. 'I thought you'd be pleased. Rowland Rawlings is influential and a word from him in the right direction would go a long way. After all, Rowland could buy his cakes from *Harrods* if he so chose.'

'So he told me,' she rejoined tartly, 'but he didn't have much say in the matter, if you're paying for this particular cake, did he? Look, Greg, I appreciate what you're trying to do, but I'm quite capable of managing my own affairs and getting my own customers.'

Greg's hands tightened on the wheel.

'Right. I was obviously mistaken to think you'd be pleased to get one or two contacts. As regards to making it on your own — well, you're not, are you?'

'How do you mean?' she demanded sharply.

'You're riding on the back of your family's reputation, aren't you? You're using the Ellises' bakery and their name.'

Eliza controlled her temper with difficulty. 'Don't be ridiculous. It's my name too. I *am* an Ellis.'

'Exactly my point! If you're going to make it on your own then you need to change your marketing strategy. Look, if you don't want to make the anniversary cake then just let me know, and I'll find someone who does

— Arthur Miller, probably. You disappoint me, Eliza.'

Greg drove in silence for the remainder of the journey and, when he pulled up at the back of the cottage, Eliza got out and didn't look back.

When she'd simmered down, though, she realised that Greg was probably right — although it was too late now. Eliza had already told the woman in the village shop who she was, and besides, it wouldn't take a genius to work it out.

*　*　*

'Greg has got a point, I suppose,' Nicola conceded, as they took another look round the empty post-office premises a few days later. 'You would be better to branch out on your own, Liza, using a different brand name for your cake-making enterprise and, one day soon, when we've got the new kitchen installed here, you'll be able to do just that. Anyway, you're still getting orders from Bembury and the surrounding district, aren't you?'

Eliza nodded. 'Ye-es, and I haven't tried anywhere in Rushden other than the local store yet. I have considered having a website, but, because I'm a one woman band, I couldn't cope with too many orders in one go.'

'You can take my word for it — Rushden doesn't know what it's missing out on, Liza! Anyway, if the locals aren't interested, there will be plenty of others who will be.'

Eliza grinned at her friend's enthusiasm. 'Good old Nicky — optimistic as usual!'

'That's me! Peter's made a good job of the paintwork, hasn't he? He's going to help with the kitchen, too.'

'It's looking great already.'

Eliza stood there trying to visualize what it would look like when the furniture was in place, with new tiles on the floor and curtains at the windows.

'I think it'll be wonderful,' Nicola put in, as if reading her thoughts. 'We're bringing my mother-in-law over at the weekend and then, once the kitchen is in and approved by health and safety, and we've sorted out all the other paraphernalia, it'll be action stations.'

'Keep me posted,' Eliza told her, feeling a surge of excitement mounting in her.

'Certainly will. I'd have told you about this enterprise way back, if I'd realised you might become involved. I'm beginning to feel really excited. And, as for your cakes, we'll find a way to promote them — even if it means a compromise for the time being.'

Eliza was peering out of the window. 'It's a perfectly ridiculous situation. After all, why should something that happened years ago have any bearing on what I'm doing today?'

'Search me! There's obviously a lot of prejudice in Rushden. Anyway, we'll show them we're a force to be reckoned with!'

★ ★ ★

That evening, James invited himself to supper.

'I've come to inspect your inheritance,' he informed Eliza when she opened the door.

'Well, you'd better come in then. You might have given me some warning. Has Leanne stood you up?'

'Absolutely not! She's having a girly night out with some mates from work.'

James followed Eliza into the kitchen and whistled.

'Wow! This is different from what I'd expected. He can't have been short of a bob or two, old Henry. It's a pity he didn't throw some of it my way!'

Eliza ignored this remark. She had already decided that if she managed to sell the pictures and one or two pieces of furniture she didn't want to keep, then she'd give the proceeds to James, but she didn't intend to tell him that just yet.

'It's cauliflower cheese for supper,' she informed him, taking a look in the oven.

James looked disappointed. 'So is this housemate of yours vegetarian?'

'No, he isn't, but Eliza and I quite like a meat-free meal from time to time,' Greg told him, appearing from the utility room with the ever-faithful Gyp in tow. He smiled, and continued, 'However, I reckon we can run to a few rashers of bacon tonight in your honour. I take it you're Eliza's brother?'

James shook the outstretched hand. 'Yep. We're not that much alike, are we?'

Greg grinned at the expression on James's face.

'You've got the same colouring. Anyway, nice to meet you. I'll have my supper on a tray, if the pair of you want to catch up, Eliza.'

'You certainly won't! James has invited himself and can take pot-luck! Look, whilst I'm cooking the bacon, why don't you show him round the ground floor?'

Over supper, James suddenly said, 'I saw your ex in town the other evening,

Liza. He asked after you. He's still with that Belinda. They'd been to some play or the other. Good thing he didn't move in here. It wouldn't have lasted five minutes!'

Eliza felt as if she were about to choke and thought of a few choice words she'd have to say to her brother when she got him on his own.

Undaunted, he continued, 'Kelvin tells me the woman who's taken over your cookery classes is an absolute dragon. Everyone's terrified of her, including the staff!'

Eliza managed a weak smile. 'I'm sure Greg doesn't want to hear all of this.'

'On the contrary, I'm intrigued,' he assured her, looking amused.

James set down his knife and fork. 'Well, you would be, wouldn't you? After all, it's your job isn't it, writing these biographies?'

'More potatoes anyone?' Eliza asked, trying to stop her brother's spiel.

They both declined and James

continued, 'So what exactly is it that you're working on at the moment, Greg?'

There was a brief pause and then Greg said, 'Oh, I suppose it doesn't really matter if you know. It's a new biography on Charles Dickens.'

'Charles Dickens!' Eliza echoed incredulously, exchanging a look with her brother who was looking equally surprised. Why on earth would Greg have wanted to make a secret of the fact that Great-Uncle Henry was writing about Charles Dickens?

Greg grinned. 'You make it sound as if it's a book about Dracula instead of Dickens,' he teased. 'Why so surprised?'

'I suppose because Henry's other books are mainly about war heroes, like Napoleon — it's just so very different from what we'd expected,' James put in.

Greg nodded. 'You're right, of course, but you see it was your great-aunt Eliza who so wanted him to write about a literary figure with Kent connections. At the time, Henry gave it a lot of thought, but because he'd gained a reputation for the type of biographies he wrote, he put the idea on hold.

'Anyway, it was his last book and it's nearly reached completion. Just three more chapters to work through. I'm beginning to see the light at the end of the tunnel.'

'OK,' Eliza said, 'but I still don't understand why you've had to be so secretive about it.'

Greg didn't answer for a moment or two and then he told her, 'It's complicated, Eliza. You probably don't know this, but your great-aunt had aspirations to be a writer herself. She'd even begun to collect some information together in an attempt to persuade Henry to write the biography.'

It was Eliza's turn to be intrigued. 'And have you been able to use it?'

'Some of it, yes, and I've had to do some of the research myself, but Henry still wrote the bulk of the book. I've been given the task of writing the preface and putting in a final chapter. Anyway, enough of that for the time being. I'd really like to sample that delicious-looking apple torte you've left in the fridge, Eliza.'

James turned to Greg. 'Before you do, there is one more question I'd like to ask. When you've finished this book on Dickens — what then?'

Greg leant back in his chair. 'How do you mean?'

'What have you got in mind for yourself? Any other work lined up?'

'There are one or two other matters that will keep me here for a while longer — if Eliza is happy to accommodate me? If not, I'll have to rethink my plans.'

Eliza swallowed, feeling acutely embarrassed by her brother's direct manner.

'James, you've said quite enough for now. Greg is welcome to stay here for as long as he needs to.'

Greg got to his feet and collected up the plates.

'Why, thank you Eliza. That's very

generous of you. On the strength of that I'll cook dinner tomorrow night.'

Eliza laughed. 'Considering it's your turn anyway, that's no big deal!'

James seemed to get on well with Greg and, after supper, he went upstairs to see the rest of the house, whilst Eliza cleared away.

Later, as they all sat drinking coffee, James remarked, 'You've fallen on your feet Eliza, and no mistake. A pity Dad doesn't see it that way.'

Eliza wished James would stop discussing family affairs in front of Greg, but she said lightly, 'He no doubt has his reasons. He found it difficult to accept that Uncle Henry sold the Rushden bakery leaving everyone high and dry, but it was all a very long time ago. Dad's just going to have to realise that I'm my own person, and I don't intend to let what happened then colour any future plans.'

'And how is the tea-shop venture?' James enquired casually.

Eliza did not look at Greg. 'Oh, that's

really Nicola's project. It's nothing to do with me at the moment, although I hope to become involved, in a small way, in the future. From what I can gather, it's gradually taking shape.'

★ ★ ★

After James had departed, Eliza and Greg went back into the sitting-room with another cup of coffee.

'Eliza, I'm sorry if I caused any problems between yourself and Kelvin.'

Eliza went scarlet. 'I've no idea why you would think that. If you must know, Kelvin ceased to be my boyfriend when I discovered he'd been two-timing me.'

'And that would have been on the occasion of the Valentine's dinner dance, would it?' he asked softly.

'Yes, actually, although why it would interest you, I've no idea.'

He reached out and placed his hand on hers.

'Of course it does, Eliza. We're living under the same roof and, even if we do go our own separate ways for much of the time, I'm not completely impervious to what happens to you. I'd be a funny housemate if I didn't care.'

Eliza caught her breath. His hand was sending a tiny shiver down her spine. She suddenly realised that she wasn't impervious to this man either. Not for the first time she recognised he was caring and thoughtful — qualities she now realised Kelvin, for all his charm, had lacked.

She wondered what had really made Greg decide to accept this post at Rushden, and was aware that she knew very little about him. Perhaps he and Natasha had needed a bit of space from working so closely with each other, and now that they had . . . ? Natasha was everything that Eliza was not: sophisticated, beautifully dressed, and obviously an astute businesswoman into the bargain.

'A penny for them,' Greg said, breaking into her thoughts.

'What? Oh, I'm sorry.' Eliza pulled

herself together with an effort, thinking it was a good job that he couldn't know what was on her mind. Instead, she asked, 'So, why exactly did you take so long before telling us about the Charles Dickens book, Greg?'

Greg rubbed his chin. 'It's complex, Eliza. You see, for a time, I couldn't locate all of the notes, and then some of them were so sketchy that I had to do further research myself. There were quite a few pages that your great-aunt had written when she had originally come up with the idea. At one stage, I wasn't even sure if it was going to work out — so what was the point in talking about it and raising people's hopes?'

Eliza was puzzled. 'But I thought you began this work when my great-uncle was still alive?'

'Correct, but you have to understand that, as he became more ill, he was able to concentrate for shorter and shorter periods. For a while I acted as his scribe, but then I encouraged him to dictate his ideas using a piece of high-tech equipment. But he had only finished about a third when he decided not to go any further, so the rest was still in note form.'

'I see,' she said, mulling this over. 'So when this book comes out, will your name be on the cover?'

'No, just mentioned in the acknowledgements. As I told your brother, I'm responsible for writing a preface and compiling a few pages at the end mentioning places to visit in Kent with Dickens connections.'

'You mean like Rochester or Broadstairs?' she asked.

'Got it in one! Now *that* section's going to involve a lot of research, as I want to visit the places concerned. For a start there's Dickens World in Chatham Dockyard.' Greg hesitated, and then said, 'I know you said a few weeks back that you'd like to help with the book. How would you feel about accompanying me on one or two of these trips? I'd welcome your input.'

Eliza's smile answered his question.

'I thought you'd never ask,' she told him, feeling that, at last, he was taking her seriously. 'Mind you, my off-duty times are a bit erratic, and once Nicola's tea-shop is open then I could be even busier.'

Greg raised his eyebrows and she could tell from his body language that he was disapproving.

'Oh, so you're still pursuing that as an outlet for your cakes, are you?'

She sighed. 'I can see I'll have to prove myself by making a good job of this cake for your friends' anniversary!'

7

Eliza arranged to visit Rowland Rawlings a couple of days later. He'd mentioned on the phone that his wife would be out shopping, and that he'd told Phoebe that Eliza would be dropping by to take another look at the outbuildings.

When she arrived at the Old Bakery, Rowland greeted her warmly.

'Phoebe's left a coffee tray ready in the kitchen, so if you'd care to do the honours.'

Eliza looked with admiration round the kitchen. She quickly found everything she needed and a few minutes later went back into the sitting-room with the freshly brewed coffee and some expensive-looking biscuits.

For a time they discussed the anniversary cake. Eliza had brought a book containing photographs of some of her handiwork to show Rowland. Apparently, Phoebe was fond of yellow, so he finally decided on a Madeira cake iced with lemon and white and with their names intertwined in the centre.

'How about a scroll design on the edge with a few sprigs of mimosa — sugar, of course — and just a hint of gold?' Eliza suggested.

'Sounds good to me,' he told her. 'I'll be a bit long in the tooth by our twenty-fifth, so I might as well make the most of this one! A tenth anniversary isn't all that inspiring — tin or aluminium, apparently. Don't fancy buying Phoebe anything made of those. Although I guess if it were you, you'd be happy with a set of cake tins!'

They laughed and Eliza thought again what a delightful man Rowland Rawlings was. Phoebe had certainly fallen on her feet when she'd come to work for him. It was obvious that he adored her.

'Well, whatever you have in mind to give her could always be wrapped in tin foil,' she said, and the elderly gentleman snapped his fingers.

'Got it in one! You know I hadn't thought of that! I've been absolutely stumped, but now you've solved my problem and I can go ahead and buy Phoebe the antique earrings she's been hankering after, and save them for this event!'

'On the other hand you could buy her a tin of biscuits,' Eliza quipped.

After they'd finished their coffee, Rowland got to his feet and they went through the conservatory and out into the garden.

'Little oasis of calm, isn't it? Strange to think of all the activity that once went on in this vicinity. I expect your father's told you a few tales?'

'Well, actually, no,' Eliza said, honestly. 'He doesn't care to talk about his life in Rushden. He was only in his twenties when he left and he's not too many years off retirement now.'

Rowland nodded. 'The years slip by somehow, especially when life keeps you busy. Anyway, I gather Phoebe didn't actually take you inside the workshop?'

'No, but she showed me the garden over there. So your house was built where the cottage once stood?'

'Roughly. There were four cottages, actually. Years back, your family lived in one and, then there were the Porters, the Coles and, of course, the Millers.'

'The Millers!' Eliza exclaimed in some surprise. 'I hadn't realised that the Millers were neighbours of my grandparents.'

Rowland smiled. 'I can see you've a lot of catching up to do. All those families I've mentioned, and one or two others, were prominent in Rushden for generations. Your great-aunt Eliza was a close friend of Daisy Miller's. In fact, everyone was friendly with everyone else in those days.'

His eyes clouded. 'But sadly, that all changed when Henry decided to sell the bakery and the entire workforce had

to find alternative work and accommodation.'

Eliza couldn't begin to imagine how
dreadful the situation must have been.
Rowland sat down on a nearby garden
seat and she perched beside him.

'So what happened to them? I mean,
I realise my Uncle Fred went abroad
shortly afterwards, and my father got a
job with the Barlows in Bembury, and
eventually bought into the bakery.
We've still got Terry Cole's daughter,
Denise, working there now. But what of
the Millers? Where did they move to? I
mean, I know roughly where Millers'
Bakery is today, but what happened
back then?'

Rowland looked at her in surprise. 'I
thought perhaps Greg or Henry might
have filled you in.'

She shook her head, wondering what
Greg had to do with it.

'My great-uncle always steered clear
of talking about the Rushden bakery
— the same as my father has done.
Most of our conversations were on

more general topics, although he did show me some photographs once. I never stayed more than a couple of hours and, for some reason, he always wanted to know what I'd been up to.'

Rowland stroked his chin. 'Yes, I suppose in many ways old Henry was a private person, particularly after Eliza died. He never came to terms with losing her — he felt so helpless. He just watched her fade away before his very eyes and was powerless to do anything. I know he got the reputation of being a bit of a recluse in later years. He came from quite a well-to-do family, you know, and he'd been in the army, which is why he was so interested in war heroes. He served with Eliza's brother — your grandfather. How's this new book progressing, by the way? Greg and Tash haven't said much.'

'Oh, well enough, I think,' she told him cautiously. 'Of course, it's bound to be more difficult without Uncle Henry being there to consult.'

'So Henry didn't ever tell you why he

saw fit to sell the bakery?'

Eliza shook her head. 'I assumed it was because he just wasn't interested in continuing with the business when my great-aunt died — too many painful memories, perhaps.'

'And you didn't ask him?' Rowland pressed gently.

'No, I was just building up to it when he became so ill, and then I lost the opportunity. Perhaps he needed the money at that time. After all, he must have spent a lot on modernising Lilac Cottage.'

Rowland Rawlings looked thoughtful. 'Yes, but that was years later. I don't think Henry was ever short of a bob or two. Well, some secrets die with the person concerned. For what it's worth, I think the same as you — that he just couldn't bear to have anything to do with this place once Eliza died. It was as if he'd somehow connected her illness with her working at the bakery. Anyway, let's take a look at the workshop, shall we? It's got one of the original bakery tables in it; the old stone floor and an oven — to say nothing of the chimney. It would have been far too difficult to get rid of it all, so the previous owners cleverly incorporated it into the garages and workshop.'

Entering the workshop, Eliza stood riveted to the spot, as she imagined what the scene must have been like when her family had lived and worked at the bakery.

Rowland Rawlings smiled at her expression.

'It's very atmospheric, isn't it? I can tell you're right back there in the time when this place was a bakery. Of course, if Greg had his way, he'd set up a little museum here, but Phoebe isn't too keen on the idea. We're working on it, Greg and me.'

'It's the first I've heard of it,' Eliza informed him, wondering what other revelations were about to be made.

Rowland leant heavily on his stick. 'Greg shares Henry's love of history. It would have been hard for Greg to have worked with him if he hadn't. Of course, with Greg, it's more local and family history that he's keen on. Why don't you ask him about it? Greg's a surprising person.'

Shortly afterwards, Eliza left. She was unaccountably annoyed with Greg. After all, the Ellises had owned the bakery long before Henry Curtis came on the scene, so anything involving her family ought to be run past them first of all.

Eliza decided to tackle Greg and find out about the memorabilia and ephemera he wanted to display. Why was he keeping her in the dark? Obviously, this was one of the matters he'd hinted at that was prolonging his stay at Lilac Cottage. However, she knew she was in for a long wait, because Greg had gone up to London that morning to call in at the publishers, and had said he'd be back late. She supposed he was dining with Natasha and found the thought disquieting.

★ ★ ★

Eliza had a chance to mull things over that afternoon during her shift at the bakery. She was working alongside Terry Cole's daughter, Denise. As they expertly iced and decorated countless miniature cupcakes and a variety of other iced fancies for the cafeteria at a local garden centre, Eliza asked Denise, a lady in her fifties, what she remembered about the old bakery in Rushden.

Denise paused in her task for a moment. 'Oh, I'm afraid there's not much I can tell you about that. I've only really known this place, and for most of the time I've worked here, it's been owned by your father. My parents told me a few anecdotes about the Rushden bakery, back before they died, but for the most part it's been forgotten. Life moves on, Eliza, and we just have to make the most of what we've got.'

She iced another row of cakes before adding, 'I do have the vaguest memory of visiting my grandparents when they were still living in that cottage in the grounds of the bakery. I can't have been any age. With a child, it's often tastes and smells that make an impression, isn't it? The smell of newly baked bread is still one of my favourites. And I do remember my mother telling me that Eliza Curtis was the most lovely, gracious lady and it was a crying shame she'd died so young.'

'So tell me what happened in the short term,' Eliza pursued. 'Did your family have to leave as soon as the bakery was sold?'

Denise picked up her icing syringe again. 'No, it didn't happen quite as drastically as that. All the tenants were allowed to continue living in the cottages until they found suitable alternative accommodation. Of course, your parents were already married and living elsewhere by then, and your Uncle Fred upped and left immediately following the announcement made by Henry Curtis. The rest of my family eventually moved away from Rushden too.'

'What about the Millers?' Eliza asked casually.

Denise deftly piped some pink swirls onto a row of cakes before replying.

'Well, the Millers were a bit different from the rest of us. You see, John Miller, Arthur's father, had always had aspirations to branch out on his own, but he didn't have the capital. His sister, Daisy, was a great friend of Eliza's and they remained friends when Eliza married Henry Curtis.

'It was through the Curtises that Daisy met her husband. He was a cousin of the family who bought the bakery. The Millers had a mysterious benefactor who helped John to set up his own bakery when Henry sold up.'

Eliza stared at Denise, trying to figure out what the older woman was telling her.

'You think this benefactor was the man who bought our bakery?'

'So it's rumoured. Of course, the

Millers never admitted to anything. I mean, it would have looked bad, wouldn't it? Everyone else had to find alternative jobs, remember. John Miller took the Porters to work with him and, eventually, there was a vacancy for my father here in Bembury. I was the only one of my sisters who continued to work here. The others had no interest.'

Eliza began to decorate another batch of cakes.

'Well, it's all fascinating stuff. I had no idea. My father's never mentioned it, and of course, the bakery here is all I've ever known. Do you happen to know the name of the family who bought the old bakery in Rushden?'

Denise frowned in concentration, but then shook her head. 'No, it's no good. It was on the tip of my tongue, but I just can't remember. They're not there now, of course. Moved some years back, I don't know what became of them. Why don't you ask your father?'

'I'm not sure that's a good idea. He's a bit touchy about the old days.

Anyway, if you remember, let me know.'

Eliza finished the final tray of cakes. 'There. All done! Tomorrow I'm going to start work on the anniversary cake for the Rawlings.'

'Did you say *Rawlings*? Aren't they the people who live in the Old Bakery now?'

'Yes, as a matter of fact. Why, do you know them?'

Denise shook her head. 'Not really. It's just that . . . I could be wrong, but . . . '

'Come on, tell me,' Eliza prompted, curiously.

'Well, I was at school with a Phoebe Porter. Her family used to work at the bakery years back, too. When she married, I gather she had a rough time with her husband and it ended in divorce. I know she went to work as housekeeper at the Old Bakery. I heard she'd eventually got married again, to her employer.'

'Yes, that's right. I've met Phoebe Rawlings. She seems very pleasant,'

Eliza replied, whilst wondering why Rowland hadn't told her Phoebe had been one of the Porters? Both he and Phoebe had mentioned the cottages, but neither of them had said that Phoebe's family had once lived in one of them.

Denise began tidying away. 'It's a small world,' she said. 'Fancy you going over to live in Rushden and being asked to make a cake for the Rawlings who live in the Old Bakery!'

'Actually the Rawlings are friends of Greg's — the chap who shares the cottage with me.'

'Really? Then I'm sure he'd know who they bought the Old Bakery from. I'd ask him if I were you.'

Yes, Eliza thought grimly. There was a lot she intended to ask Greg Holt about.

* * *

Eliza didn't catch up with Greg until the following morning, when she

206

encountered him in the kitchen scrambling eggs and grilling bacon.

'Ah, good. I've done enough for two. I've no idea why going up to London makes me so hungry.'

'Greg, I need to talk to you before you disappear into the study again.'

He peered into the saucepan. 'That sounds ominous. What have I done — forgotten to clean the bath?'

'Don't be facetious!' She was not in the mood for his banter.

He set her breakfast down and said, 'So come on — tell me what's on your mind. I've obviously done something to upset you, but I can't put it right if I don't know what it is.'

'This idea of yours about setting up a museum at the Old Bakery. Why didn't you see fit to mention it to my family?'

He looked at her in surprise. 'Oh, so Rowland's told you about that, has he?'

A prickle of annoyance made her say curtly, 'Why wouldn't he? Or is this another of your little secrets?'

Greg's eyes widened. 'I thought

207

you'd be up for it.'

Eliza poured herself some more coffee.

'Oh, you did, did you? If that were the case, then you would have discussed it with me before now. You really do like to take things upon yourself, don't you?'

He sighed. 'It was only an idea and, of course, I realise your family would need to be consulted. When I was going through Henry's papers in the study, I came across a few things relating to the bakery that must have belonged to your family.'

She stared at him, open-mouthed. 'You've got a nerve! You had no right going through anything other than papers relating to the book you're working on!'

'Eliza Ellis! You are the most exasperating woman at times,' Greg said loudly. 'How on earth am I supposed to differentiate between pages from Henry's manuscript and pages relating to the bakery, unless I sort through them? So, please, feel free to come and do it yourself. You've indicated you wanted to help, so here's your opportunity. There are other items too, and I've put everything into a case as I've found it.'

Eliza's cheeks were slightly pink, as she realised perhaps she'd been a little hasty with her accusations. They finished their breakfast virtually in silence.

Eliza was upstairs in Henry's room when there was a tap on the door. Greg stood there with a battered old suitcase in his arms.

'There's no time like the present. This contains most of the items you wanted to see. Apparently, there's some more stuff in the attic at the Old Bakery. It was rescued by the previous owners. I'm sure Rowland would be only too glad if you took it off his hands. So, where do you want this?'

Eliza felt foolish. 'I didn't mean to offend you, Greg, but I can see that I have.'

He shrugged. 'Just dented my male

ego a little, maybe. I was convinced you'd think the museum was a good idea, but perhaps I was being a bit high-handed.' He indicated the case. 'Anyway, it's up to you what you want to do with this little lot now.'

And, before Eliza could think of a suitable reply, he had set the case down, stalked off along the landing and disappeared into the study again. She stood staring after him, realising that he had somehow managed to make it seem as if she was the one who was being unreasonable.

★　★　★

Eliza had arranged to meet up with Cynthia, Nicola and Martin at the tea-shop that morning. She had an hour or so to spare before she needed to be there and so, heaving the case into the room, she curled up in the big old armchair and quickly became immersed in the contents.

There were several notebooks full of

handwritten recipes, receipts and order books, cash books and a bundle of letters. There were also a number of photographs and inventories. Digging to the bottom of the case, Eliza found several aprons and caps, presumably belonging to her great-aunt, and some rather delightful posters and postcards.

Eliza was just about to have a word with Greg when she heard his car start up, and remembered he'd said he was going out that morning. She felt disappointed, but it would have to wait.

★ ★ ★

She was a bit late arriving at the tea-shop. Nicola's mother-in-law, Cynthia, was deep in conversation with her son and daughter-in-law. They looked up with a smile as she entered.

'Oh, good, you've made it!' Nicola greeted her. ''Fraid the men came early though, so you've missed our discussion. Everything's going ahead as planned. The new kitchen goes in at the end of next week and then, hopefully, it'll all be plain sailing after that.'

'Isn't it exciting?' Cynthia Bligh beamed. 'I'm so looking forward to getting stuck in. It's good that you're going to join us, Eliza.'

'Well, if my cake-making enterprise doesn't take off as well as I've anticipated, then I might be donning an apron and serving teas,' Eliza remarked.

'Oh, it'll all come together, you'll see,' Nicola said, with more optimism than Eliza felt. 'Once this place is up and running we'll soon earn a reputation.'

'But, in the meantime, I need to earn some money,' Eliza pointed out. 'I had no idea how expensive running a home was going to be.'

'Welcome to the real world, my dear,' Cynthia said in her forthright manner. 'Anyway, I understand you've got a lodger so that must help with the expenses.'

'Yes, but he isn't exactly a lodger. I inherited Greg along with the cottage.

It's complicated.'

Cynthia looked mystified. 'Sounds a strange arrangement to me. Now, who's for a cup of tea? I'm sure Eliza's dying to see the up-to-date plans. After all, it's the pair of you who are the experts when it comes to deciding how the kitchen should be.'

Excitedly, Nicola and Eliza pored over the plans.

'How much space d'you think you'll need, Eliza?' Nicola asked.

'Oh, not too much to start with — just enough to advertise and show photographs of my work, and a few shelves for the decorations that can be housed in baskets initially . . . '

As they chatted, Eliza suddenly felt much more positive about her new project than she had done for the past few weeks.

Whilst they'd been talking, Martin had taken himself off to the pharmacy, butcher's and general stores to find out if they were any happier about the presence of the tea-shop now that it was more of a reality. He was gone for quite some time.

'So?' Nicola asked when he returned. 'What's the verdict?'

Martin considered. 'I think we're beginning to make progress. It seems that whilst folks are bitter about the loss of the post-office, they realise it was inevitable. Apparently, there's some discussion about setting it up elsewhere in the village. I reckon the natives are willing to be friendly, providing we tread carefully.'

'Some folk just don't know where they're well off,' his mother told him. 'When you think what these premises might have been used for . . . '

'Oh, I think we'll win them round once they see how good the place looks,' he assured her. 'Mind you, I'm afraid it's a bit of a different story in the general stores. It seems the lady Eliza spoke to is related to the couple who used to run the post-office, and she reckons it's shades of the bakery closing all over again.'

'She's far too young to remember that,' Eliza said.

'Seems her grandfather worked there when he was a boy. She says if it hadn't been for the Millers, things would have been very difficult when everyone got laid off practically overnight. That's why folk around here are so supportive of them. They've got long memories.'

'Would you rather I pulled out now?' Eliza asked him peevishly, suddenly weary of the whole affair. 'I mean, if it's going to cause so much bad feeling for the rest of you.'

'No you won't! We need you!' Nicola told her fiercely. 'You're not getting cold feet now. We're going out to lunch and you're coming with us. You're one of our team!'

They enjoyed a pleasant lunch in the local pub and, over the meal, Eliza found herself relaxing. She returned to Lilac Cottage with a much lighter heart. Going into the garden she sat on the swing under the old apple tree, and that was where Greg found her ten minutes later.

'How's your day been?' he asked.

'Great, thanks. Yours?'

He came behind her and, catching the swing, gave it a push, as if she was a child.

'Fine thanks, as business meetings go. Look, Eliza, about this morning. I didn't mean to upset you.'

'I've told you, it's OK,' she assured him. 'In fact, it's more than OK. Now that I've had the time to think about it, the museum is a great idea — preserving things for posterity.'

He steadied the swing and she scrambled off and turned to face him, giving him the full benefit of her smile.

'I was just being daft. The stuff in that case is amazing! I can't wait to look at it in more detail, so thanks, Greg, for sorting it out. Someone else might have thrown it away.'

And, on an impulse, she caught his hands between hers.

For a moment his grey eyes locked

216

with hers and then, suddenly, she was in his arms and he was kissing her. She was filled with a kaleidoscope of emotions.

'I suppose I ought to apologise, but I've wanted to do that for a very long time,' he told her softly. 'If your great-aunt was anywhere near as enchanting as you are, Eliza Ellis, then I can quite understand why Henry was so enamoured with her.'

A deliciously warm feeling encompassed Eliza. Her heart was pounding and she knew that things would never be the same between them again.

'Flattery will get you everywhere,' she told him lightly, her eyes shining.

'Can I take you out this evening to make up for my high-handed attitude this morning?'

'Love to, but I'm a working girl and I've got a late-night shift,' she told him, regretfully.

He nodded, looking disappointed. 'Another time, then? That's if you want to.'

Her heart sang. 'Yes, Greg, I do.'

It was beautiful in the garden. The apple blossom was out and the flowerbeds were a mass of colour. Eliza spotted a cluster of feathery fronds and, following her gaze, Greg said softly, 'That'll make a lovely show when it comes out — the love-in-a mist.'

* * *

The next few days passed by in a whirl. Eliza had thought herself in love with Kelvin, but he hadn't had the effect on her that Greg was having. She told herself to take things slowly and not get too carried away. After all, she'd only just got over Kelvin, and Natasha was still very much there in the background. Perhaps Greg was feeling lonely and fancied a no-strings-attached fling. Well, he'd chosen the wrong person if he did!

She immersed herself in her work at the bakery, taking on a few extra shifts for a lady whose husband was recovering from an operation. This, along with her own cake-making enterprise, meant Eliza didn't have much time for herself.

On Friday night, Greg sought her out as she unloaded some shopping in the kitchen.

'Ah, you're back! I was beginning to think you've been avoiding me. I was wondering if you wanted to go out for that meal tonight? I'm a bit tied up for the remainder of the weekend.'

Eliza's first reaction was to refuse. It was such a casual invitation, and she'd had a long day but, in spite of all her misgivings, she found herself accepting.

She dressed carefully for her evening out in a midnight-blue, sleeveless dress, twisting her unruly locks into a loose top-knot. She was glad she'd made the effort, for Greg looked extremely elegant in dark trousers and jacket with a lilac coloured shirt.

The restaurant he took her to, deep in the heart of the Kent countryside, was smart and overlooked a stream.

'Wow!' she exclaimed, as they studied the menu over drinks in the bar. 'This place is quite something.'

'My cousin recommended it. He's been here a few times.'

Eliza looked at him in surprise. 'Oh, I didn't realise you had any relatives in this area.'

A curious expression crossed his face. 'Yes, there's a cousin of my father's and his wife and their two sons. Dale's married and lives in Staplehurst, near Maidstone. Brendan lives with his parents, a few miles out of Rushden.'

'Right — and your parents?' She realised she knew very little about him.

'Oh, my parents and sisters live in Sussex. We moved there when I was around ten.'

At that moment they were told that their table was ready and, after they'd ordered, Greg asked, 'So, how's the cake progressing for the Rawlings' anniversary?'

Oh, fine. It'll be all right on the night,' she assured him with a grin, then went on, 'Changing the subject — if we go ahead with this idea of the museum,

I suppose there'd need to be a lot of discussion. I mean, I don't know how one goes on about doing something like that.'

'I think it's a case of first things first,' he told her. 'If we can collect enough memorabilia and ephemera from folk who had ancestors at the bakery, then that's a good start. I appreciate there are a number of issues — insurance, for one — but I'm sure Rowland Rawlings has the right contacts to deal with such matters. Let's just play it by ear, shall we?'

Over the meal, the conversation changed to more personal topics, such as their taste in music and reading, plays they had seen and exhibitions they'd visited recently. They found they had a lot in common.

'I can see that we've both got similar tastes in art,' Greg smiled. 'Perhaps we could grab some free time and go to see an exhibition together?'

'I'd like that very much,' she told him, eyes sparkling. She felt that their relationship was taking on a new dimension.

As they sat over coffee in the elegant lounge, Eliza wished the evening could go on for ever. All too soon, however, they returned to Lilac Cottage. As they walked along the path he took her arm in his and it seemed the most natural thing in the world.

Once inside, Eliza began to thank him for the evening, but he caught her in his arms and silenced her with a kiss that took her breath away. She responded in kind, nestling close to him. He set aflame every fibre of her being.

The telephone ringing, shrill and relentless, broke into their private world.

Greg hurried into the hall to answer it and Eliza heard him say, 'Tash — I hadn't expected to hear from you this evening! Thought you were busy. Is everything OK for tomorrow?'

His words were as effective as if she'd been under a cold shower. She suddenly came to her senses and shot up the stairs and into her room. She was right. He had been amusing himself at her expense, because Natasha had been occupied. The weekend for him would begin the following day!

Tears blurred Eliza's eyes as she got ready for bed. Why did she always choose to fall for the wrong man? Her cheeks burned as she remembered how eagerly she had returned his kisses. She was going to have to keep her emotions under a tight rein in future.

8

Sleep evaded Eliza that night and so she decided to get up at the crack of dawn. After showering she went downstairs, intending to take Gyp for his walk, but it seemed Greg had beaten her to it. She was pushing a piece of toast around her plate when he entered the kitchen, Gyp following in his wake.

'Good morning,' Greg said pleasantly. 'You're up with the lark.'

'I've a lot to do,' she rejoined tartly. 'There's tea in the pot and I've made too much toast.'

'Thanks. I was wondering if you could see to Gyp for the rest of the weekend? I was going to ask you last night, but you'd disappeared by the time I'd finished my call.'

'And why should that surprise you?'

She'd heard him calling goodnight from outside her door, but had pretended to be asleep.

Greg hesitated. 'Look, about last night ... I'm afraid I must have misread the signals. If so, then I apologise. It won't happen again. I'm away for most of the weekend and then, if you want me to move out, I'll understand.'

She nodded, not trusting herself to speak. He hadn't misread the signals, but she had no intention of letting him know that. As for him moving out, she didn't want that, but it wouldn't hurt him to think she was considering his suggestion.

'I'll look after Gyp,' she told him, 'although I'll be at the bakery some of the time.'

He stood there for a moment, looking as if there was something else he wanted to say, but in the end he changed his mind.

As soon as he'd gone, Eliza wanted to call him back to put things right between them, but pride wouldn't let her.

* ★ ★

At the bakery that morning, Eliza put the finishing touches to a fiftieth birthday cake. She had to admit she was pleased with the result. She looked up with a smile as her father came into the room.

'Still here? Don't you know all work and no play makes Jill a dull girl?'

'Actually, I went out last night and this cake needs finishing. The birthday party's this evening at the village hall, and I'm off to deliver it presently.'

Roy came to stand beside her.

'You're looking a bit peaky, love. Are you eating properly?'

'I'm quite capable of looking after myself, Dad,' she told him. 'Anyway, in case you've forgotten, I'm having my Sunday lunch with you tomorrow. Mum's doing roast chicken. There is just one thing though. I'm looking after Gyp for the weekend. Greg's away and . . . '

'You want to bring Gyp along? The

more the merrier, I would have thought. Tell you what, how about I come and collect the pair of you? It's about time I took a look at this cottage you've been raving on about for so long.'

For a moment Eliza couldn't believe her ears, and then she let out a delighted yell and kissed her father on the cheek. It was early days, but perhaps she could win him over after all.

* * *

The following morning, Eliza walked Gyp, breakfasted and went to the service in Rushden church with Nicola and her mother-in-law. Afterwards, when Nicola and Cynthia were chatting to an acquaintance, Rowland Rawlings sought Eliza out.

'How's the cake coming on?' he asked conspiratorially.

'It's all in hand,' she assured him. 'Do you want it delivered on Saturday or before?'

'Oh, bring it with you when you come to the party, my dear. That will be time enough.'

'Oh, but I hadn't expected . . . ' she floundered in embarrassment.

'You haven't received the invitation?' he boomed. 'I expect Greg's carrying it around in his pocket. Where is he this morning?'

'He's away for the weekend,' she informed him, aware that Nicola was watching them with interest. Eliza was grateful when Rowland nodded, excused himself, and crossed to talk to someone else.

'What party?' Nicola asked, as they walked through the churchyard.

Eliza filled her in briefly, adding, 'I really don't want to go. I won't know anyone and it's totally out of my league.'

Nicola shot her a surprised look. 'That's not like you. You're always such a good mixer — wait a minute, have you fallen out with Greg?'

'No . . . Well . . . we've had a bit of a

228

misunderstanding, that's all. I'm beginning to think it's not such a good idea him living in Lilac Cottage, after all.'

Nicola's eyes widened. 'Really? Whatever's happened? Is it that girlfriend of his?'

But Eliza had absolutely no intention of telling her friend anything and, fortunately, at that moment, Cynthia caught up with them and they changed the subject.

★ ★ ★

Eliza was in the garden, watching out for her father. As he came along the path, she got to her feet, suddenly feeling like a young child again, waiting for his approval.

'What a pretty garden, Eliza,' he said. 'So, where's this mutt?'

She opened the back door and Gyp came rushing out of the utility room to greet them, tail wagging ecstatically.

Roy Ellis quickly made friends with the animal and then stood looking around the kitchen in surprise.

'My goodness, Liza. This is a bit different from how I remember it! I'd no idea there'd been so many improvements.'

'Mum said she'd tried to tell you, but you just weren't interested,' Eliza pointed out.

Roy Ellis looked a little awkward. 'No, well, I'm afraid she was right there. Anyway, perhaps it's time to forget the past and move on. Life's too short to dwell on things that happened years ago.'

'Do you want to see the rest of the cottage?' Eliza asked him tentatively.

'Oh, come on then. It's a strange feeling, being here after all this time. Where did you say this lodger of yours is today?'

'I'm not too sure,' Eliza told him. 'Off enjoying himself with his girlfriend, I shouldn't wonder. She was Henry's editor, Natasha Milton. It turns out she's related to Phoebe Rawlings, who lives at the Old Bakery now.'

Her father pursed his lips. 'You don't say! Didn't your mother tell me you're making a cake for the Rawlings' wedding anniversary?'

'Yes, as a matter of fact, it's my project for next week. No good starting on it too early because it's rich Madeira — not fruit. Come on, let's have a look around or we'll be late for lunch.'

Eliza's father approved of the décor in the other rooms on the ground floor. She had mastered the entry system to the study and took him to see that next. Gyp followed them upstairs excitedly, obviously thinking that Greg might be there.

Roy was suitably impressed. 'My goodness, Liza. This little lot must have cost a tidy packet. I wonder what Aunt Eliza would have made of it all!'

'From the little I've gleaned about her, she'd have been very happy. She was all for progress.'

'Hmm! Well it's just a pity old Henry couldn't have seen fit to pour some of his money into the Old Bakery instead of selling it. It was badly in need of modernisation from what I remember. Anyway, it's too late in the day now . . . Steady, boy!'

Gyp had been wagging his tail so hard that he'd dislodged a pile of papers and pamphlets from the desk, and they fell to the floor with a thud. As Roy Ellis stooped to pick up one of the books, a piece of paper fluttered out and he retrieved that too. It turned out to be a bookmark. Turning it over, he read the handwritten message frowningly and, opening the book, stared at the name written on the inside cover.

'Dad, I'm not sure we ought to be doing this,' Eliza told him, uncomfortably.

'In the circumstances I think I can be forgiven. Well done, dog, for drawing this to my attention!'

'What are you talking about, Dad?' Eliza peered over his shoulder and read the name aloud. 'Daisy Miller — that's interesting. She must have given the book to Great-Aunt Eliza.'

Her father shook his head. 'Not so. Look at the message on the bookmark.'

As she read it, her eyes widened in disbelief. 'I don't understand.'

The words sprang out at her, as she tried to make sense of them.

Dear Greg,

I thought you might like to have this book as it belonged to your grandmother. Kind regards, Arthur.

Eliza gasped. 'But that can't be right. Greg's surname is Holt, not Miller!'

'And Holt was the name of Daisy's husband — a relation of the man who bought the bakery from Henry.'

Eliza stood staring in stupefaction at her father for several minutes. Gyp whined and she patted him absently.

'But you didn't say anything when I mentioned Greg's name before.'

'I did to your mother, but she thought it was just a coincidence. After all, it's not an uncommon surname and Greg was working in a London

233

publisher's when he met Henry, didn't you say?'

Eliza nodded, feeling numb. 'Greg has tried to warn me off attempting to sell my cakes round here, and he didn't think the tea-shop was a good idea either. Why on earth wasn't he upfront with me from the beginning? If only he'd told me about his family connection with Millers' bakery, I might have understood.'

Her father sighed deeply. 'I think the most likely explanation is that he wanted to test the water first. After all, you might have shown him the door from the outset, and it's obvious he's keen to finish this project. It just goes to show that my instincts were right all along.'

'So how do you make that out?'

'Well, it stands to reason, Liza. Greg will support Arthur Miller because he's a member of his family. Greg knew you wouldn't empathise with him and he's obviously keen to sort his own life out with the least possible hassle. No, I reckon you'd have done better to have sold up, love.'

Eliza swallowed hard. 'I suppose Greg must have his own reasons for keeping quiet. He's never questioned me about our bakery, but I have discussed a few things with him about my own projects and aspirations. He could have passed them on to Arthur Miller, if he so chose. How could he deceive me like this?'

'Perhaps I ought to have a word with Arthur Miller — see what he's got to say,' her father mused. 'I mean there's always been a bit of rivalry between the two of us, but we're not arch enemies or anything. Anyway, it's no good brooding. Of course, we could just keep quiet — wait and see what transpires. But right now, we need to get back to Bembury or your mother will be champing at the bit.'

As they passed Greg's room, Eliza tried the door handle but, as usual, it was locked.

'D'you know I've never been invited

to take a look at Greg's room. Now I'm beginning to wonder if he's got family photos or suchlike in there, and he doesn't want me to make the connection between himself and Arthur Miller.'

Her father frowned. 'Well, he must have realised you'd be bound to find out sometime, love, so you're just going to have to confront him with it!'

The knowledge that Greg had been deceiving her upset Eliza more than she had thought possible. Whatever his motive, she now felt as if she couldn't trust him any longer.

By the time she had arrived back at Lilac Cottage that evening she'd made a decision. Gregory Holt was going to have to finish Great-Uncle Henry's book elsewhere!

★ ★ ★

There was a message from Greg on the answer phone. Eliza listened to it twice before deleting it.

'I've decided to stay with friends for a couple of days, Eliza. We both need a bit of space. I'll be back in time for the Rawlings' party. I gather you haven't received your invitation. Apparently Rowland gave it to Natasha to give to me, but she forgot and has been carrying it round in her handbag for days.'

So that explained one thing at any rate, although Eliza wouldn't have put it past Natasha to have hung on to the invitation deliberately. Eliza didn't know what to do. Should she go to the party and endure seeing Greg with Natasha? It seemed a bit churlish to refuse the invitation and, after all, Rowland seemed intent on mending bridges — unless, of course, he just wanted to see how Eliza's cake-making matched up to Arthur Miller's!

Meryl Ellis hadn't seemed too surprised when her daughter had mentioned Greg's relationship with the Millers.

'In the same way that there's a

striking resemblance between yourself and Aunt Eliza, there's certainly a family likeness where Greg and his grandmother are concerned. The other day I came across an old photograph taken at the Rushden bakery. Actually, it was in that bag of memorabilia you gave me to look through belonging to Aunt Eliza.'

'Humph,' Eliza grumbled. 'Well, I've got more important things to do with my time than waste it thinking about Greg and his schemes.'

Try as she might, however, she could not get Greg out of her mind. She missed his company, and Gyp was obviously pining for him; he took to sitting on guard outside the study door for much of the day and whining pitifully. Eliza soon realised that she wasn't so keen to be at Lilac Cottage on her own as she'd thought. It was such an old cottage that it had its own noises — especially in the dead of night. Eventually, she allowed Gyp to sleep in her room.

She made the Rawlings' cake at the beginning of the week and began to ice it on the Wednesday. She had already made most of the floral decorations in readiness.

Later that day, Nicola invited Eliza to take a look at the new kitchen at the tea-shop, which was well on its way to completion.

'It's brilliant! You'll be in operation sooner than I could ever have believed possible.'

'Told you so. Right, now I need your opinion on the colour for the walls and the flooring. Martin's really tied up at the moment so he's left it to me, and Cynthia isn't bothered one way or the other — although she did say nothing too garish, like orange or purple!'

'Personally, I was going to suggest sky-blue pink,' Eliza said, keeping a straight face.

'What! Oh, be serious, Liza!' Nicola laughingly nudged her friend in the ribs. 'I can't have you telling me you refuse to work in the kitchen because of the colour scheme!'

The two girls spent a while looking at the paint charts and finally agreed on a colour scheme.

'You know how Greg arranged for your carpet to be fitted?' Nicola said over coffee. 'Well, I was wondering if his mate also did flooring.'

'Oh, Greg's away at the moment. Actually, Nicky, there's something I'd better tell you. It's not working out too well — us sharing Lilac Cottage. He might be moving out sooner than I expected.'

'I see,' Nicola said, and looked at Eliza, head on one side. 'There's definitely something you're not telling me, isn't there, Liza?'

Eliza shook her head, wishing Nicola wasn't quite so observant.

'No, just that. Look, he's due back any time, so why don't you ask him yourself?'

'There are times, Eliza Ellis, when I could shake you!' her friend told her. 'You don't want to let a guy like Greg escape so easily, you know.'

'Even if he *is* related to Arthur Miller?' Eliza asked her quietly.

Nicola stared at her friend in disbelief. 'You're kidding me!'

'I only wish I was, but it's true. It seems Arthur's aunt Daisy, who was a friend of my great-aunt's incidentally, was Greg's grandmother.'

'That sounds ridiculously complicated, so I'll just have to take your word for it. Exactly how long have you known all this?'

'Since Sunday.' She filled Nicola in briefly.

Nicola whistled. 'Well, that explains a lot of things. At least, I think it does! Why on earth didn't he tell you himself, instead of being so mysterious?'

Eliza shrugged, wishing she knew the answer to that herself.

'Perhaps he thought I'd throw him out on his ear? After all, there's always been a bit of competition between the two bakeries. Each one wanting to out-do the other. I suppose it's all rather silly really, but neither side seems prepared to climb down.'

'Perhaps this is the turning point, Eliza. After all, you've never been involved personally, so why not take a stand? Say you're not prepared to put up with all this rivalry and nonsense and that's an end to it once and for all!'

'Yes, I'm sure you've got a point. I don't see why my entire future plans should be jeopardised because of something that happened before I was born.'

Nicola clapped her hands. 'Phew, that's a relief! For a while there, I thought you were going to give in to them. The sooner this tea-shop's opened, the sooner we can start promoting your products!'

'Great! Let's get this show on the road.'

* * *

Eliza spent the afternoon at Lilac Cottage doing some costing for some customers' orders and had just decided she needed a well-deserved cup of tea when the doorbell peeled shrilly. She thought Greg must have forgotten his key but, to her amazement, she found Kelvin standing on the doorstep looking rather awkward. He was the very last person she had expected. She stood staring at him for a moment, wondering why on earth he was there.

'Hallo, Liza. I hope you don't mind me cold calling. I wanted to ask you a favour. I bumped into Jamie in town. He said he thought you'd be working from home today.'

'You'd better come in,' Eliza said rather stiffly. 'If you go into the sitting-room I'll get you a coffee.'

But Kelvin followed her into the kitchen and perched on a stool as she made the drinks.

'OK,' she said, placing a mug in front of him and putting a plate of tray-bakes within easy reach. 'So what is it you want to ask me?'

'My cousin Tracey's getting married

. . . You remember Tracey?'

Eliza wrinkled her brow. 'Vaguely — wasn't she a bridesmaid at your sister's wedding?'

'That's the one. Well, my mother was so impressed with the cake you made for Angela that she wondered if you'd make one for Tracey. Mum wants to give it to her for a present. I know it's a bit awkward, but I said I'd ask you. After all, you can only say no.'

'What do you take me for, Kelvin?' Eliza demanded. 'Just because you and I have broken up, it doesn't mean to say that I'm going to cold shoulder your entire family.' Her eyes widened. 'Oh, wait a minute; you were hoping I'd give you a discount, weren't you?'

'If you could, that would be much appreciated,' he said honestly, 'but, if not, I'll understand.' He took a large gulp of coffee before adding, 'I had hoped we could still be friends.'

'When you're looking for a favour,' she told him coldly, and was gratified to see the colour rise to his cheeks.

She sighed. 'Oh, go on then, for old time's sake.'

'Thanks, Liza. I know roughly what she wants — got it here somewhere.'

He scrabbled about in his pocket and extracted a scrap of paper.

Eliza gave it a cursory glance. 'Yes, that seems fine, but I'll need to liaise with you again. Although it would make more sense if I had a chat with Tracey. I'll ring you when I've got some designs to show her and I'll do some costing, too. Now, tell me all the hot gossip from school.'

Kelvin was just doing an impression of Mrs Mitchell at the last staff meeting when Gyp began barking excitedly. A few moments later the back door opened and Greg came into the kitchen carrying a huge bouquet of flowers. He stopped short at the sight of Kelvin, muttered something and disappeared into the utility room followed by an ecstatic Gyp.

'So that's the guy you're house-sharing with! Who's the lucky lady?'

Kelvin's eyes widened and he looked at Eliza incredulously.

'It's you, isn't it? Well, he's got it made, hasn't he?'

Eliza's cheeks flamed as she realised that Greg must be able to hear all of this conversation. She got to her feet, not trusting herself to speak for a moment or two.

'You've got it all wrong!' she told him icily. 'How dare you jump to conclusions!'

Kelvin grinned infuriatingly. 'If you say so! I believe you — thousands wouldn't!'

There was a silence, during which Kelvin got up and reached for his jacket.

Just then Greg came out of the utility room, looked at Kelvin, extended his hand and said pleasantly, 'I don't believe we've met. I'm Greg Holt.'

'Yes, I know who you are,' Kelvin rejoined, 'and I expect you're aware that I'm Kelvin Summers. I'll be off then, Liza. Will you be in touch regarding that little matter we were discussing — when you've had a chance to think about it?'

Eliza nodded and followed him to the back door. After he'd gone she remained there for a while, breathing deeply and trying to compose herself.

Greg had vanished again, but reappeared presently with the flowers.

'Eliza, I can only apologise. I had no idea you and Kelvin were back together again and he's obviously misconstrued the situation. I bought these as a peace offering — that's all. I realise I owe you an apology for the way I behaved last week. Now it seems I've only made matters worse, but it was truly unintentional. Anyway, perhaps we can put them somewhere neutral, like the hall or the upstairs landing.'

'Don't be so ridiculous! It would be an utter waste of good flowers,' Eliza told him, taking the offending bouquet from him and sniffing the blooms.

Presently she looked up and gave a little smile.

'Apology accepted. They're gorgeous. I'm afraid Kelvin's renowned for opening his mouth and putting his foot in it. As for us getting back together again, he and I are history, Greg.'

'Really? Well, that's a relief — I mean I'm sorry you've split up, but at least I haven't been the cause of it happening all over again.'

'Don't think you've earned yourself a reprieve,' she informed him sternly. 'I accept your apology, but there's another matter we need to discuss, as I'm sure you're aware — something you ought to have told me right from the outset.'

Greg looked puzzled. 'And what might that be?'

'Don't play the innocent with me, Gregory Holt. I've had more than I can take of all this deceit for now. In fact, I've had enough of men altogether!'

And she stormed out of the room leaving Greg to stare after her in bewilderment. Eliza Ellis was a spirited young woman, as he'd noted before, and he admired her for that. It was a pity that she seemed to think they were on a different wavelength, because he was becoming increasingly fond of her.

He racked his brain, trying to work out what he'd done to upset her now, but couldn't come up with an answer. Shrugging, he went to fetch his case from the car. Perhaps the only solution would be to move out of Lilac Cottage, but that wasn't really an option just now.

*　*　*

Eliza was kept so busy for the next day and a half, decorating the Rawlings' cake and finishing others, all for delivery at the weekend, that she didn't have time to dwell on her problems.

Greg behaved impeccably, obviously keen to dispel any notion she might have had that he had any romantic intentions towards her. He cooked the supper on Thursday evening — a very tasty chilli and rice — worked like a Trojan in the garden and did a big shop on Friday morning.

'OK,' she told him, as he stashed the food away in the fridge. 'You've done your penance — don't labour the point! Come and have a look at the Rawlings' cake. See if it meets with your approval.'

She lifted the lid of the box and he peered at the cake for so long that she wondered if it wasn't quite what he'd expected. At length he touched her gently on the shoulder.

'Eliza, you've excelled yourself. It's magnificent! I couldn't have done a better job myself!'

Catching sight of the twinkle in his eyes, she burst out laughing. He was incorrigible and, try as she might, she couldn't remain cross with him for long. If only he wasn't involved with Natasha Milton . . . and why, oh why, hadn't he mentioned he was related to Arthur Miller?

'D'you think they'll like it?' she asked, when she'd sobered down.

'Like it — I should jolly well hope so!

Those sugar flowers round the outside are so realistic I could almost pick them! Yes, it's a triumph!'

'As good as Miller's bakery could produce?' she asked, wickedly.

'Equally.' And then, seeing her expression, he asked, 'So, how did you find out?'

She told him, adding, 'When exactly did you propose to tell me you were related to the Millers — to say nothing of the Holts who bought the bakery from Uncle Henry?'

Greg looked awkward. 'Oh, I was just waiting for the right moment. So far as I'm concerned, it's no big deal what happened all those years ago between the prominent families in Rushden. I was aware I'd have to mention it before tomorrow evening, because Arthur and Polly Miller will be at the Rawlings' do. In case you haven't worked it out, Arthur's my father's cousin.'

He ran a finger through his hair. 'Look, I may be Daisy Miller's grandson, but that's no reason why the

251

two of us should fall out. After all, your great-aunt was a good friend of hers and I don't have any issue with that.'

Eliza closed the lid of the cake box. 'The fact remains that you've not been open with me, Greg. My father still feels awkward about what happened to all those families when Uncle Henry sold the bakery.'

'Your father's obviously an honourable man. As you're no doubt aware, he vowed never to encroach on Arthur's territory or to do anything to put his business in jeopardy again. He's stuck to that promise over the years and Arthur's done the same for him. But you, Eliza, have stepped in where angels fear to tread, because you feel it's time to move on. If you remember, I tried to dissuade you, as I'm aware people around here have long memories. But then I decided it might be an idea to support you instead, which is partly why I asked you to make Phoebe and Rowland's cake. Obviously, that was a mistake, because you've been listening to your father and you've been having second thoughts.'

Eliza shook her head. 'It's nothing to do with that. Of course, I think it's time to move on and put all this stupid rivalry behind us. No, what's disappointed me is that you didn't explain why you objected to me setting up in business round here. I suppose you thought that by keeping me in the dark, your home here would be safeguarded.'

Greg looked totally taken aback. 'That's a bit below the belt, Eliza! I've got a job to do and, when it's finished, I promise I'll leave you in peace, but until that time, d'you think we can call a truce and try to live in some kind of harmony?'

'That's all very well,' she said, heatedly, 'but you can't just expect me to forget the way you've behaved. How do I know you aren't harbouring any more secrets?'

'I assume that applies to both of us,' he told her, tight-lipped. 'When you've

253

calmed down and are prepared to think about the situation, then I think you'll agree there's absolutely nothing to get so steamed up about.'

And before she could think of a suitable reply, he had gone.

Eliza sank onto the kitchen stool, trying to regain her composure before going out on her delivery round. She was far too angry to get behind the wheel of her car. Who exactly did Greg think he was? He always seemed to get the upper hand and make her feel as if she was the one in the wrong.

She supposed that, at the end of the day, it didn't really matter that he was related to Arthur Miller and she was an Ellis. If Greg — aware of all the feeling in the community — had been prepared to work for her great-uncle, then why couldn't she put the past behind her too? The problem was, it wasn't that simple where Greg was concerned.

Suddenly Eliza made up her mind. She was going to have to tell the Rawlings she couldn't attend their anniversary celebration after all. She picked up the phone, but only managed to leave a message with the daily help.

9

Rowland Rawlings was waiting for her when she arrived at the Old Bakery. To her relief, he was delighted with the cake.

'My dear, that's quite splendid! Phoebe will be over the moon.'

'Tell me, Mr Rawlings, does she think you've ordered a cake from Arthur Miller?'

He shook his head. 'All she knows is that it's Greg's present to us — which is very generous of him. Now, I know you're driving, but I've got some non-alcoholic wine. Come and sit down and talk to me for a few minutes. Phoebe's busy with one of her charity dos and I'm in dire need of some company.'

As they sat sipping the fruit wine, they chatted about Rowland's plans for the museum. Suddenly he said, 'Now, tell me what's troubling you, my dear. I'm well aware that something is.'

Without meaning to, Eliza found herself telling Rowland Rawlings about how she felt an outsider in Rushden because she was an Ellis, and that now she'd discovered Greg was related to the Millers, she felt even worse about the situation.

'It was lovely of you to invite me to your anniversary celebration but, under the circumstances, I feel it would be best if I didn't come. I don't want to cause any bad feeling on your special day.'

There was a silence during which Rowland studied his hands and appeared deep in thought, and then he looked up.

'It's all too easy to get bogged down with silly, petty issues. There are far too many real disasters in this world at present: wars, earthquakes, famines and floods — to say nothing of the problems with the global economy. So why, oh why, are we worrying about trampling on one another's toes over selling a few bakery products, or who did what to whom, all those years back? It isn't important, Eliza. Now, I want both you and Greg to be at our party tomorrow and to have a thumping good time. And if you don't put in an appearance, then I shall personally come and fetch you, is that understood?' He raised an eyebrow, then continued, 'I'm getting a bit long in the tooth so I like my own way and, I might add, I'm used to getting it! It's high time the Ellis family became a part of this community again.'

Eliza smiled. 'And that's just fine, so long as folk round here are prepared to accept that. But I could get weary of hanging about waiting for it to happen.'

He gave her a searching glance. 'You could, but you won't, will you, Eliza? Because you're like your aunt Eliza, whose namesake you are. You've got spunk and won't give up easily.'

★ ★ ★

'So,' Greg said over breakfast the next morning, 'Did Rowland like the cake or shouldn't I ask?'

'Well, seeing as you're paying for it, of course you can,' she told him, buttering a slice of toast. 'He was delighted — said it was just what he'd wanted for Phoebe. I understand that Arthur Miller is catering for the rest of the buffet.'

'Is he? I wouldn't know. I don't see him that often. Do I take it you're coming after all?'

'How could I refuse when Rowland was so persuasive? But, don't worry; I'll be on my very best behaviour. You can introduce me to all your relatives and I'll be perfectly polite.'

He laughed. 'Relax — apart from the Millers there won't be anyone else from my family there. My parents are visiting one of my sisters in Derbyshire, who's just had a baby, and my other sister's on holiday in Spain. The relative who once lived in the Old Bakery died a long time ago, and his family live in the

United States nowadays.'

'Right, I'd best get on,' Eliza said briskly, gulping her tea and collecting her dirty crockery. 'I've a million and one things to do this morning.'

'I'll see you this evening then,' he told her, and she nodded.

★ ★ ★

By later on that afternoon, Eliza was heartily wishing she'd invented a previous engagement. The last thing she wanted was to make polite conversation with a lot of people she'd got no intention of socialising with again. However, by the time she'd had a long soak in the bath and washed her hair, she felt considerably better. She was undecided what to wear and, in the end, chose a summer dress in shades of pastel green. She coiled her shining fair hair high on her head and secured it with diamante pins.

Raking through her jewellery box, she found some dangling jade earrings and a necklet to match. A pair of silver sandals completed her outfit. Her make-up was minimal and she sprayed a little light perfume behind her ears. Sweeping up a white wrap and silver bag, Eliza came out of her room at precisely the same moment as Greg appeared from his.

He whistled appreciatively. 'Wow! You'll steal the show tonight. You look a million dollars, if I'm permitted to say so.'

Eliza coloured slightly. 'Of course,' she rejoined lightly, her heart thumping wildly. 'I'm not impervious to a little flattery now and again. And — if I might return the compliment — you're looking pretty good yourself.'

He was wearing a beautifully-tailored grey suit and a pale blue, open-necked silk shirt. This man was seriously good-looking, thought Eliza; and she was not impervious to that, either.

Greg inclined his head. 'Thank you, fair lady. I meant to ask you if you'd like to have a lift with me. I've arranged for a taxi so that I can enjoy a drink, and it seems daft to take two cars to the same place,' he said casually.

She hesitated. 'Oh, but I thought . . . That is, what about Natasha?'

He frowned. 'What about her?'

'Well, I mean . . . ' she floundered, 'doesn't she need to be picked up from somewhere?'

'Not this evening. She's already at the Rawlings' helping Phoebe to get things organised. Tash is a great organiser.'

As Eliza leant back in the rear seat of the taxi, she was extremely aware of the man sitting beside her. She could smell the fresh fragrance of his cologne; see the way his rich, dark hair curved into the nape of his neck. If only they could begin again without all those misunderstandings — and without Natasha — perhaps their relationship could become something more than this rather confusing friendship.

The drive was already packed with cars. Suddenly feeling apprehensive,

Eliza accompanied Greg up to the house, wondering what was in the small, gift-wrapped box he was clutching. She suspected it was something more expensive than the rose vase she had bought the Rawlings, and Greg had already paid for their cake.

The front door was flung open and Natasha stood there looking amazing in a clinging coral pink dress that must have cost a fortune. Her hair had golden highlights and her makeup was perfection.

'Greg — at last! Where have you been, darling?' She gave Eliza a forced smile. 'Hallo Eliza. So you've decided to come, after all. I must introduce you to one or two people.'

Eliza was beginning to wish she hadn't come when Rowland caught sight of them from his post just inside the sitting-room door and waved.

'Eliza, my dear, and Greg. Come along in.'

The room was filled with groups of people. Everyone seemed to know everyone else and there was a hubbub of voices.

'Come on, I'll get you a drink,' Greg said, and steered her towards a waiter who was carrying a tray full of fluted glasses of wine.

'Oh, but I don't expect you to stay with me,' Eliza protested. 'Natasha's been waiting for you.'

'What? Oh, she's far too busy acting as hostess. Phoebe is probably still organising the caterers. Periodically, she still slides back into her role as housekeeper — can't help herself. Ah, there she is, talking to Arthur. Probably congratulating him on the buffet.'

Phoebe Rawlings, looking elegant in a white dress, was deep in conversation with a portly gentleman whom Eliza vaguely recognised. He looked up as they approached.

Greg propelled her forward. 'Hallo Phoebe, many congratulations. Arthur — here's someone I'd like you to meet. This is Eliza Ellis.'

Arthur Miller's rather florid face

creased into a smile and he extended a hand.

'My, you've grown a bit since I last saw you. Looks like I'm going to have to watch my back. I can see I'm up against some strong competition. Your cake is certainly a fine specimen. You've got your aunt Eliza's skills. Mind you, we haven't sampled it yet, and the proof of the pudding is definitely in the eating!'

'Oh, I'm sure you'll find it tastes as good as it looks,' Greg told him.

Arthur Miller's eyebrows bristled. 'And just whose side are you on? Anyway, we've provided some tortes which are to die for, so I'll expect you to sample those and give me your honest opinion, young Eliza, and I'll do the same with yours!'

'Stop teasing the poor girl, Arthur,' Phoebe said. 'I'm sure all the food will be delicious. Now Eliza, come with me and I'll introduce you to someone who's also on his own.'

A sandy-haired young man was

standing in a corner nursing his drink and Phoebe introduced him as her nephew, Phil. Eliza realised, at once, that she would have absolutely nothing in common with him. He stared dolefully into his glass and told her that he was going through a particularly sticky divorce, and that it had taken some persuasion on Phoebe's part to get him there at all.

Eliza tried to be sympathetic as she listened to his tale of woe, but was heartily relieved when someone tapped her on the shoulder.

'Eliza Ellis, what on earth are you doing here?'

Spinning round, she found Bob Holmes and his wife Chris, who both worked in the art department at the high school Eliza had recently left.

Bob gave her a smacking kiss on the cheek.

'We miss you — and we miss those scrumptious cakes you used to provide us with at staff meetings!'

'He's always thinking of his stomach,'

his wife teased. 'Rumour has it you made that wonderful-looking anniversary cake for the Rawlings.'

'Yes, I did, as a matter of fact.' Eliza was uncomfortably aware that she was standing within earshot of Arthur Miller and his family.

'Our daughter's eighteenth birthday is coming up soon — can we press-gang you into making her cake?'

'I'd be only too delighted, Chris. Let me give you my card.'

Eliza scrabbled in her bag, conscious that Arthur Miller was watching her. Any minute now he would pounce and tell her she was poaching on his territory.

'You and Chris must come over to supper some time.'

'Of course, you've moved into Lilac Cottage. I'd heard you were living in the vicinity. We'd love to come, wouldn't we Bob? But perhaps we'd better leave it 'til the holidays now. You know how frenetic the end of term is, and things don't get any better.'

Just for a moment, Eliza felt a pang of nostalgia, and a sudden desire to be a part of that crazy world again.

'Anyway, how come you're here tonight?' Bob asked.

Eliza smiled. 'Courtesy of the cake. Greg Holt introduced me to the Rawlings.'

'Oh, of course — Greg. Didn't someone tell me you're sharing the cottage with him?'

'Yes, he's a sort of unofficial lodger,' Eliza explained briefly and then asked, 'So, what about you two?'

'Chris is distantly related to the Porters,' Bob informed her. 'Phoebe was a Porter before she married Rowland. In fact, at one time, the Porters used to work in the bakery at the back here and live in one of those cottages that were pulled down. It's a small world, isn't it?'

'Come to think of it, didn't your family used to own the bakery here once upon a time?' Chris asked.

Eliza nodded. 'Yes, years back, and

then my great-uncle Henry sold it to the Holts, who built this house.'

'Oh, yes, of course, Greg's a Holt. But the ones who lived here weren't his immediate family, were they?'

'Apparently not, although Daisy Miller — who married a Holt — was his grandmother and Arthur Miller's aunt.'

A glazed expression came over Bob's face. 'Fascinating as all this family history is, can we leave it there, because I'm starving and they tell me there's a fantastic buffet awaiting us in the marquee. Why don't you join us, Liza? We'll fill you in with all the gossip from school — or Chris will!'

Fortunately, the sandy-haired young man had moved away to speak to the Millers, and so Eliza joined Chris and Bob. They selected a table in the marquee and then went to queue for some food.

Eliza was relieved to have found some friends she knew to talk to, rather than having to spend the entire evening making polite conversation with strangers.

As Bob had said, it was a wonderful spread, with a centrepiece of fresh salmon and various meats, salads and game pie, together with a variety of other individual savoury delicacies that Arthur Miller had provided. A number of waitresses stood around the tables waiting to assist.

As they sat down with their laden plates, Chris indicated the table at the top end of the marquee.

'Look, the dignitaries are over there!'

Eliza followed her gaze and saw the Rawlings surrounded by a number of people she didn't recognise. Chris and Bob filled her in just as Arthur Miller and his sons joined the table, followed by Natasha and Greg. As Eliza watched, she saw the way Natasha was looking at Greg, at one point placing a hand possessively over his.

'He's good-looking, isn't he, your lodger?' Chris commented, giving her friend a keen look.

'Well, yes, I suppose he is.' And Eliza realised that she resented the way Natasha was making sheep's eyes at Greg.

Eliza concentrated on her food, interested to taste what Miller's had provided for the buffet. She had to admit that it was good, although somewhat different from the fare that Ellis's bakery would have offered.

Presently, she and Chris sampled a piece of the strawberry torte Arthur Miller had also provided. They both agreed it was sumptuous.

As folk finished eating, there was a stir from the top table and Rowland Rawlings rose to his feet, banging the table for silence. He made a delightful little speech about being happily married for ten years and finished by saying:

'And now it's time for cake and champagne. This oh-so-beautiful cake was made by the young lady hiding herself away at the far end, there. After all these years, it's my great pleasure to

271

welcome the great-niece of Eliza Curtis, nee Ellis, back to the Old Bakery. Incidentally she's also called Eliza Ellis!'

Eliza felt the colour rise to her face. The glasses were filled by an army of waiters, the cake was served by a procession of waitresses and the toasts were made to Phoebe and Rowland Rawlings.

To Eliza's great relief, her cake was a success. The rich, buttery Madeira was just as she had hoped and she received a number of compliments.

After coffee, she was glad to escape into the garden. It was a balmy June evening. The garden was illuminated by fairy lights strung from the trees and a quantity of solar lights on the edge of the lawn. Soft music filled the air and couples began to drift out of the marquee.

Eliza sank thankfully onto a seat beneath an arbour of roses, breathing in their heady perfume.

'Ah, there you are! What are you

doing lurking out here on your own?' Greg asked, and sat down beside her.

'I'm not lurking,' she told him. 'I came out for a few minutes' peace and quiet.'

He chuckled. 'Yes, it can be a bit overpowering — all that chatter. The Rawlings have a lot of friends and relations between them. I saw you were stuck with Phil for a while, earlier on. Poor soul — he's always looking for a fresh ear to bend about his problems . . . I didn't realise you knew Bob and Chris Holmes.'

'It's a school connection,' she explained. 'It was good to meet some folk I know amongst all this crowd.'

'Yes, I'm sorry to have deserted you. Peaceful spot you've found out here.'

They sat for a time in companionable silence, preoccupied with their own thoughts.

'It's strange to think that my great-aunt must have often walked in this part of the garden,' Eliza said, presently. 'I do so wish I could have met her.'

'Mmm, I suspect you'd have got on pretty well together. I reckon she'd have been tickled pink to think we're both living quite amicably under her roof, and that we're attending a party here tonight in the grounds of the Old Bakery.'

He paused and then said: 'I've just got a little more to do on the Dickens book. I was wondering if you might consider coming to Broadstairs with me?'

'Broadstairs!' she echoed. 'Why Broadstairs in particular?'

'Well, there's Bleak House, of course, but apparently, your great-aunt was very fond of Broadstairs and so I thought . . . '

Eliza smiled. What harm could it do — to spend time in the company of a man she was becoming increasingly fond of? She knew Greg had only asked her because of her relationship to Eliza and Henry Curtis, but it would be lovely to spend a whole day with him. She met his questioning gaze.

'Yes, I'd love to. Perhaps in the middle of next week?'

'Greg! I've been looking for you all over the place!'

Natasha stood looking at the pair of them, as a head teacher might survey a couple of naughty school children playing truant. She pointedly ignored Eliza and, catching hold of Greg by the arm, said impatiently, 'Come on, the band's arrived and the dancing's about to begin!'

Reluctantly, Eliza followed them back inside. All the tables had been moved to the edge of the marquee, leaving a large space in the centre.

To her embarrassment, Arthur Miller beckoned her across to where he was sitting with his wife and a large carbon copy of himself.

'This is my son, Brendan. He helps me in the bakery whilst my other son, Dale, is an accountant and manages the financial side. He's over there dancing with his wife, Mandy. I've been looking for you, young lady. I've got a proposition to put to you. And, afterwards, Brendan can give you a spin round the dance floor.'

Brendan grinned amiably at her. It seemed his father's word was law.

'Just look at Greg and Natasha — make a handsome young couple, don't they?' Arthur remarked.

Eliza mumbled something which she hoped was appropriate, wishing she didn't have to watch the two of them. She realised with a start that that she was feeling jealous. With an effort, she forced herself to concentrate on what Arthur Miller was saying.

'You know, I think I've come up with a solution which could benefit the pair of us, young Eliza. That cake you made has certainly passed the test . . . so, how would you feel about joining forces with me and working as part of my team at Millers' Bakery?'

This was the last thing Eliza had expected. She was silent for a moment or two, wondering how to reply and not knowing whether to laugh or be furious.

At last she said carefully, 'I'm flattered you should ask me, Mr Miller, but I already work part-time for my father, quite apart from running my own cake-making enterprise.'

Arthur Miller grunted. 'So you're turning me down, lass? A pity; I thought it would solve all of our problems.'

She stared at him. 'How do you mean?'

'Well, you're obviously keen to spread your wings and I'm looking for fresh talent to expand my business. Not only that, but I've heard on the grapevine that you're planning to take your cake-making and sugar-craft expertise into that new tea-shop opening in the old post-office!'

'Did Greg tell you that?' Eliza demanded indignantly.

He chuckled and tapped his nose. 'My lips are sealed, but I have my informants. My customers are loyal and, if you worked with me, you'd get paid a good salary. But if you attempt to go it alone then you could come badly unstuck — that's all I'm saying, lass. So don't be too hasty to refuse. Come back to me by the end of next week, shall we say?'

Keen to get away from him without any unpleasantness, Eliza reluctantly agreed.

During this conversation, Brendan had been standing by his father's side, smiling infuriatingly. Now he grabbed hold of Eliza's hand and, pulling her onto the dance floor, twirled her round. He reminded her of an energetic puppy and he reeked of pungent cologne. Her head was in a whirl, but she was grateful to escape from Arthur Miller.

'You mustn't mind Dad,' Brendan told her. 'He likes having his own way and you're the first person in years he's seen as serious competition. He's met his match!'

'Who's been talking to him about the tea-shop? That's what I'd like to know.'

Brendan shook his head. 'You'll soon learn that everyone round here knows everyone else's business — at least, they think they do. You know, if you came to work at Millers' I guarantee you'd enjoy it and . . . ' he paused significantly, winked and tightened his grip on her waist, 'we could see more of each other. I'd like that!'

Eliza felt like screaming. She had enough problems as it was, without unwanted admirers.

They finished the dance and, much to her relief, Greg came across to her.

'Come on, Eliza!'

'Are we going home?'

'Not until you've danced with me!'

Her heart lurched. As he whisked her onto the floor he said, *sotto voce*, 'You looked in dire need of being rescued. My cousin's a nice enough chap, but he can be a bit overpowering, like his father.'

Eliza nodded. 'Actually, his father has just offered me a job at Millers', and I'm not too sure what to make of it!'

She studied Greg's face, but his expression gave nothing away.

'Is that so? Well, I'd congratulate myself, if I were you. You must have made quite an impression. There's been no end of compliments flying around tonight. It would seem people are genuinely delighted that you're here, representing the Ellis family.'

'I suspect that was your doing, Greg,' she said unsteadily. 'And, no doubt, you've been talking to Arthur Miller, too. Don't think I'm not appreciative, but I'm quite capable of standing on my own two feet. The tea-shop is due to open very shortly and I've every intention of providing the cakes and making no secret of where they came from, either!'

Greg smiled. 'Good for you. And contrary to what you might think, I haven't been bending Arthur's ear on your behalf. I suppose the culprit might be your friend's mother-in-law. Phoebe tells me Mrs Bligh's recently joined the Rushden WI and that's a hot-bed of gossip.'

Eliza's cheeks flamed. 'I'm sorry,

Greg. I shouldn't have accused you. I was just a bit taken aback, that's all. I suppose I ought to feel honoured, but it's put me in a dreadfully difficult position.'

'It's your choice. I can't see you allowing anyone to pressgang you into doing anything you're not happy about,' he said with a smile. 'Now, let's enjoy the rest of this dance, shall we?'

Over his shoulder, Eliza could see Natasha dancing with Brendan Miller. Greg was a good dancer and she began to relax. The touch of his hand on her waist made her catch her breath and her heart began to pound wildly.

Eliza was suddenly aware of Natasha glancing in her direction, as if to say, 'Hands off my guy!'

As the dance ended, she came across and took Greg's arm possessively.

'Come on, Greg. It's my turn again now. One dance with Brendan is quite enough. I've done my duty.'

Eliza sank down on a chair, wishing she could go home, but realising she was stuck until Greg decided it was time to leave. She was aware that someone had come to sit beside her and, turning her head, saw it was Rowland Rawlings.

'Everything's going splendidly, isn't it? Phoebe's having a ball. I couldn't have wished for anything better. You don't look as if you're enjoying yourself, though. You don't want to mind Natasha, you know. She manages to get her own way in most things, but just don't let her get away with it.'

Before Eliza could reply, some guests came across to say that they had to depart. She was left puzzling over Rowland's remark.

Natasha could certainly dance and she and Greg looked good together. At that moment, Eliza heartily wished she'd never set foot in Rushden because then she wouldn't have met Greg, who was doing strange things to her heart.

★　★　★

They hadn't been back at Lilac Cottage many minutes when the phone rang. Greg had taken Gyp out for a quick walk and so Eliza answered it.

A woman's voice said urgently, 'It's Penelope Lewis. You must be Eliza. I've been trying to get hold of Greg all night.'

'We've been out at an anniversary party,' Eliza told her. 'Can I give him a message? He'll be back shortly.'

'Tell him to contact me on my mobile. It's his father-in-law. He's had a massive heart attack!' And she rang off.

Eliza just stood there, staring at the phone, as the woman's words sank in. Just then Greg appeared in the doorway.

'Someone called Penelope Lewis has just rung,' she said tersely. 'Apparently, she's been trying to get hold of you all night. Can you phone her back on her mobile? It seems your father-in-law's had a massive heart attack.'

Without saying a word, Greg raced to

the phone and a minute or two later she could hear him talking in soothing tones to the woman at the other end.

Automatically, Eliza removed Gyp's lead, hung it up and settled him for the night. She was making coffee when Greg returned.

There were to be no explanations just then, however.

'Penny needs me to be there as soon as possible. Can you ring for a taxi? I daren't drive — too much to drink. The number is in the book.'

Greg took the mug of coffee Eliza handed him and raced upstairs to reappear, less than ten minutes later, with an overnight bag.

'Liza, I know I owe you an explanation, but it's going to have to wait. Don needs me right now!'

He bent and kissed her on the cheek just as the car turned up.

10

The following morning Eliza awoke unrefreshed, as if she'd had an unpleasant dream, and then she remembered.

Greg hadn't denied that he had a father-in-law, and who *was* Penelope Lewis? Eliza felt bewildered, and angry with Greg. Why couldn't he have been straight with her? She ought to have realised that something had driven him to bury himself in Rushden. And what about Natasha? Was she the cause of the break-up of his marriage?

With a jolt, Eliza suddenly realised why she was so angry, and sat staring out of the window at the lilac tree. She was in love with Greg Holt. Could life get any more complicated for her?

★ ★ ★

Greg's father-in-law did not survive the night. Greg rang to say he'd be staying with Penny, whoever Penny was, until her brother arrived from Ireland.

Later that morning, Eliza joined her mother for church in Bembury.

Meryl looked at her daughter with concern.

'You're looking pale, darling. Of course, it was the Rawlings' party last night, wasn't it? How did it go?'

Eliza told her briefly, steering clear of what had happened afterwards.

'Well, I'm glad the cake was a success. Strange to think you've been to the Old Bakery, after all these years.'

'It's totally different now, of course. There are just a few relics of the past in the outhouses as a reminder of bygone days, but there's a lot of atmosphere when you're in the garden.'

Eliza was spared any more questions as the service began at that moment.

★　★　★

For the next couple of days, Eliza threw herself into work at the bakery. As well as fulfilling orders for her own enterprise, she covered for one of the staff, who needed time off because she had friends staying from America.

The problem was, Eliza still had time to think and there was no-one to confide in about this particular problem. She didn't know how she was going to face Greg when he returned.

Nicola rang, telling Eliza that the kitchen had passed the inspection and that, apart from a few minor jobs, everything should be up and running within a couple of weeks. She asked Eliza if she could spare the time to meet her at the tea-shop that afternoon.

Eliza was delighted with the finished kitchen. It was everything she could have dreamed of. The oak-effect furniture and pale blue floral tablecloths, seat-covers and curtains gave the tea-shop an air of old world charm which was in keeping with the age of the building. In the corner was a large Welsh dresser.

Cynthia pointed to it smilingly. 'That's where we thought you could display your sugar-craft items. It's only a small place to begin with — just until things take off.'

Eliza stared at her friends in surprise. 'But I thought you wanted me to wait for a bit.'

'Change of plan. We've decided to start as we mean to continue. We're going to have a good advertising campaign and you're having a mention,' Nicola told her firmly.

'We're going to have small vases of fresh flowers on every table,' put in Cynthia, 'and on the walls, there's going to be a bit about the history of the building and some photographs of the post-office as it used to be in its heyday.'

Nicola grinned at her. 'We're having some menus printed and, on the back, we intend to advertise your cake-making and sugar-craft.'

'Just hold on a minute,' Eliza pleaded. 'My head's spinning with all this information!'

She told them about Arthur Miller's offer and how she didn't want to tread on his toes.

'No problem. We can get round that one,' Nicola assured her. 'You specialise in cakes and, as you've already said, your father wouldn't wish to encroach on Miller's territory — although both Cynthia and I think that's ridiculous. Anyway, we're considering asking Miller's to provide the bread for our sandwiches, together with some rolls. That should solve the problem, shouldn't it?'

Eliza pulled out a chair and sat down.

'It's certainly a compromise, and I admit I'd prefer to concentrate on providing the cakes.'

Nicola beamed. 'OK. Let's seal the deal with a nice pot of tea and some of those wonderful tray-bakes you've brought along.'

The following evening, Eliza was watching a film on TV with Gyp stretched out in front of her, when Greg returned. She thought he looked incredibly tired and drawn and longed to throw her arms about him, but knew it wouldn't do, Instead she greeted him coolly.

'How are things?'

'Oh, we're coping, thanks. It's always a difficult time, but Alec's there now — Don's son. I couldn't leave Penny to deal with things all on her own.'

'Who *is* Penny?' Eliza asked curiously.

Greg looked startled. 'Didn't I say? She's Don's daughter — my sister-in-law. She's absolutely devastated, as you can imagine.'

Eliza nodded and went off to the kitchen to return shortly afterwards with a pile of ham sandwiches and some coffee. Greg certainly had a lot of explaining to do, but right now, he looked in dire need of sustenance.

'Thanks, Eliza. Food hasn't exactly been my first priority, as you can imagine.'

She couldn't look at him and swallowed hard.

'Greg, you owe me an explanation. All these weeks I've thought you were single, and suddenly I learn you're married. Where's your wife?' she asked, coming straight to the point.

He gulped down a sandwich and washed it down with coffee. Eliza waited.

'Tessa — my wife — died a few years back. I thought perhaps Rowland had told you, but he obviously hasn't. You must have wondered why I chose to bury myself away here and, if you'd have asked, I would have told you. Athough I still find it difficult to talk about.'

Eliza stared at him, trying to get her head round this. She had gone from thinking he was single, to imagining him separated, and now she realised he was a widower.

She put a hand on his arm. 'I'm so sorry, Greg. I didn't mean to be intrusive. Naturally, I wondered what really brought you to Rushden, but I assumed it had something to do with Natasha.'

He swallowed some more coffee before looking up.

'Ah, yes. Natasha,' he said, and didn't deny it.

She tried again. 'I really don't want to pry, Greg, but your wife — was it an illness?'

He shook his head. 'I might have been able to accept it a bit more if it had been. We'd gone down to Devon for a few days. Tessa loved horses and there were stables nearby. She was an experienced horsewoman, but her mount was highly strung. There was a sudden storm and the horse bolted and threw her.'

He paused and she could see how painful the memories were for him.

'Normally it would have been OK,

but there was something wrong with her riding hat — it wasn't fastened securely and it came off. You can work out the rest.' He lowered his gaze and continued in a barely audible voice. 'It's taken me a long time to come to terms with what happened and to move on. Don, my father-in-law, found it impossible. I've tried to be there for him ever since, and to support him in whatever way I could and, you see, Natasha's been there for me — a tower of strength these past years.'

'Yes,' Eliza said quietly, 'it must have been a terrible time for you and your wife's family. What a dreadful tragedy! It's good that Natasha's been there for you.'

A strange look flickered across his face.

Eliza gathered up the plates, refilled Greg's cup and went out to the kitchen. Her heart was full. Of course she sympathised with Greg, but she realised now that Natasha had been by his side when he'd been going through this ordeal, and that was why she was so close to him.

'Do I take it that's why you've never wanted to show me your room — perhaps because of photographs you've got there?'

'Got it in one — almost, anyway.' He picked up his bag. 'Come on, I'll show you now.'

There was a large, framed portrait on the wall of an attractive, dark-haired young woman.

'That's Tessa. A friend of ours painted it and Tessa gave it to me on our first wedding anniversary.'

Eliza saw the sadness in his eyes. As she stood gazing at the portrait, she decided that the sooner Greg went from her life the better. She had to accept that she could never win a place in his heart and that she didn't deserve to.

Greg returned to Hertfordshire the following week for the funeral and, when he came back to Rushden, their relationship was one of companionable friendship once again.

* ★ ★

The official opening of the tea-shop was a great success. Cynthia had come up with the idea of having it on the same day that Rushden had a garden safari, and offered to do a special deal on the teas, with a generous percentage going to church funds. This took the pressure off the organisers who could now relax and enjoy the occasion.

Arthur Miller provided sandwiches and sausage rolls, Cynthia and Nicola made mountains of scones, whilst Eliza contributed oceans of tray-bakes, iced fancies and tea loaf.

Eliza also donated a cake as a raffle prize, and Arthur Miller supplied one of his famous pork pies. He put in an appearance halfway through the afternoon and beamed at the customers.

'You know, lass,' he said, turning to Eliza, 'perhaps this isn't such a bad idea, after all.'

Eliza pretended she didn't know what he meant and he winked at her.

'You're a chip off the old block and no mistake. Us working alongside each other is what I meant, as you're well aware!'

Eliza had invited her parents but hadn't really expected them to show up, so when they did, she was delighted. They congratulated Nicola, Martin and Cynthia and walked across to examine Eliza's sugar-craft display and the cake she'd made for the raffle.

When she looked up from speaking with a customer, Eliza found her father deep in conversation with Arthur Miller.

She had just handed a small boy a couple of cupcakes, when Greg came into the shop.

'Thought I'd pop by to see how you're doing.'

'Fantastically,' Eliza assured him, her heart beating a wild tattoo. 'This was an absolute brainwave on Cynthia's part! That's my father over there talking to Arthur Miller.'

He took her arm. 'Wonderful! Come

and introduce me.'

To Eliza's great relief, Arthur and her father seemed to be getting on like a house on fire.

'Hello you two,' Arthur boomed. 'Roy, this is my cousin's son, Gregory Holt — Daisy Miller's grandson. When I first heard he and Eliza were going to be sharing Lilac Cottage, I thought, now there'll be fireworks; but they seem to be muddling along OK.'

Roy Ellis nodded and shook Greg's hand. 'I must admit I didn't like the idea of Eliza being there on her own,' he told him. 'It's good to know there's someone to keep an eye on her.'

Eliza didn't dare to meet Greg's gaze. Her father just wouldn't accept that she was quite capable of looking after herself.

'This young daughter of yours is as talented as her great-aunt,' Arthur proclaimed loudly. 'Of course, it might be a different matter when it comes to pies!'

Fortunately, Greg stepped in just

then, skilfully directing the conversation back to the purpose of the afternoon: raising funds for repairs to the church tower.

When the rush of visitors had died down, everyone took it in turns to have a look at some of the gardens. Greg offered to walk round with Eliza.

It was still sunny and the gardens — each with their own blend of individuality — were a riot of summer flowers and perfumes. Eliza bent to sniff an apricot rose.

'Perhaps next year, if they have another garden safari, we could let people take a look at the garden at Lilac Cottage,' she suggested.

Greg gave her a curious look and the colour flooded her cheeks, as she realised that he'd probably be moving back to London soon, and out of her life.

'Were you thinking of employing me as your gardener?' he teased gently.

'I was just day-dreaming,' she rejoined, thinking it was the euphoria of the afternoon that was having such an effect on her.

They wandered into a secluded part of the garden. The scents from the honeysuckle and orange blossom were intoxicating.

'Eliza, I was wondering . . . '

'Yes?' She met his grey eyes questioningly. She was standing so close to him that she fancied he must be able to hear how rapidly her heart was beating.

'There have been so many misunderstandings between us, Liza. We got off on the wrong foot. Do you suppose we could start afresh — get to know each other a bit better?'

She smiled at him, incapable of speech, and suddenly, she was in his arms and he was kissing her in a way that left her in no doubt as to what he meant.

$\star$ $\star$ $\star$

'Come and look at this, Greg!'

Eliza was reading some diary entries

in a notebook of her great-aunt's, which she had discovered amongst the memorabilia Greg had given her. Coming into the room, Greg sat down in Henry's armchair.

'What's the matter? What have you discovered?'

'It's this diary entry of Great-Aunt Eliza's. Just listen to what she's written.'

Greg leant forward, eyes alight with interest, as Eliza began to read from the faded book.

'*I feel certain my illness has got something to do with my work at the bakery. It feels as if the very life-blood is draining away from me. Ironic when I consider how much I used to love working there, but now I detest it. The doctors won't listen to me, but I feel sure that I'm right.*'

'Well, there's one way to find out. Let's do a bit of research on the internet,' Greg suggested.

It didn't take long for them to find a website on food allergies and intolerances. It could never be proved, but they soon realised there was a strong possibility that Eliza Curtis had been suffering from coeliac disease, a condition that had made her sensitive to the gluten in wheat and other cereals. This would undoubtedly have been greatly aggravated by her work at the bakery. If untreated, it could have been a cause of her premature death.

All this gave Eliza a lot to think about, and she suddenly had the idea of producing gluten- and wheat-free products for the tea-shop, and adding them to her celebration cake range. It would mean doing some more research, but she was prepared to do just that.

★ ★ ★

The next few weeks passed in a whirl. Eliza and Greg went to Broadstairs during the Dickens festival, taking part in the fun. As they strolled around, arm in arm, picking out the various characters from Dickens' books, Eliza wondered if her great-aunt and uncle had done the same thing.

'I promise we'll come here again when it's quieter,' Greg told her.

She nestled against him as they stopped to watch the Dickensian bathing party on the beach.

'I'd like that, but this is great fun too!'

'So, we're following in your great-aunt and uncle's footsteps, as well as those of Charles Dickens. They all enjoyed holidaying in Broadstairs!'

Eliza paused to take some photographs of characters from *The Pickwick Papers*.

'If I close my eyes, I can almost imagine my great-aunt and uncle are down there on the beach, enjoying a picnic and listening to the banjo playing.'

Greg laughed. 'You understand why I so wanted to continue with this book, then?'

'Yes, everything makes perfect sense now. Oh, Greg, thank goodness I didn't sell Lilac Cottage!'

Greg put an arm about her waist and pulled her close.

'Lilac Cottage is a very special place so, if you had put it on the market, I'd have made you an offer you couldn't have refused. But then I wouldn't have got to know you, would I?'

Presently, Eliza said, 'So have you got all the additional material you need to finish the book?'

'Oh, yes, it's virtually done. I discussed the final details when I visited the publisher's last week. And the other tasks — sorting out Henry's manuscripts and setting his writing affairs in order — they're almost finished too.'

'But what about the museum? You are still going to help with that, aren't you?' she wanted to know.

He looked amused. 'If you'd like me to, but there's no real rush, is there? Actually, there's something I need to tell you. You know I've been offered another job — back at the publisher's?'

She nodded and he squeezed her hand. 'Whilst I was in London last week, I had a heart-to-heart with Natasha.'

Eliza met his grey eyes uncertainly, wondering what she was about to hear.

'Tash tells me she's decided to take a career break — join her family in Spain, just until she's sorted her life out. Unfortunately, it seems she'd hoped we . . . Well, that we could be more than good friends.' Greg sighed. 'I'd no intention of hurting her. I offered to turn down the job and look for work elsewhere, but Tash had already made up her mind to leave. Shades of you and Kelvin.'

'No, Greg,' Eliza assured him firmly. 'Since I've met you, I've realised I never really loved Kelvin. There's only one man in my life and I'm looking at him right now.'

'That's just as well,' he teased gently, 'because I've got absolutely no intention of sharing you with anyone!'

Her heart had plummeted when he'd mentioned Natasha, but now it seemed to be beating uncontrollably.

He tucked her arm in his. 'Liza, when you came to live in Lilac Cottage a few months ago, we made an arrangement. You said you agreed to my staying there until I'd finished Henry's book, together with the other tasks he'd asked me to complete. I like to think I keep my word, and so it's almost time for me to move on.' He turned to meet her gaze. 'That is, unless . . . '

'Unless?' she prompted, her green eyes looking at him questioningly.

'Well, if you were to invite me to remain at Lilac Cottage then I might be persuaded to do so, but it would need to be on my terms this time round.'

'And what would they be?' she asked softly, her pulse racing.

'That you agree to marry me, of course,' he replied, smiling at her tenderly.

'Oh, yes, please,' she told him, her heart singing. She caught his hand. 'Come on, let's go home. We've got a wedding to plan!'